P9-EJT-510

| WALKING ON WATER

CALGARY PUBLIC LIBRARY

AUG - - 2010

CALGARY PUBLIC LIBRARY

AUG - - 2010

| WALKING ON WATER

JANCIS M. ANDREWS

Stories

Cormorant Books

Copyright © 2009
This edition copyright © 2009 Cormorant Books
This is a first edition.

No part of this publication may be reproduced, stored in a
retrieval system or transmitted, in any form or by any means, without the prior
written consent of the publisher or a licence from The Canadian Copyright
Licensing Agency (Access Copyright). For an Access Copyright licence,
visit www.accesscopyright.ca or call toll free 1.800.893.5777.

 **Canada Council Conseil des Arts
for the Arts du Canada**

ONTARIO ARTS COUNCIL
CONSEIL DES ARTS DE L'ONTARIO

The publisher gratefully acknowledges the support of the Canada Council for the Arts
and the Ontario Arts Council for its publishing program. We acknowledge the financial
support of the Government of Canada through the Book Publishing Industry Development
Program (BPIDP) for our publishing activities.

Printed and bound in Canada

Library and Archives Canada Cataloguing in Publication

Andrews, Jancis M. (Jancis Maureen), 1934–
Walking on water / Jancis Andrews.

ISBN 978-1-897151-17-4

I. Title.

PS8551.N372W34 2009   c813'.54   c2007-906477-9

Cover design: Angel Guerra/Archetype
Text Design: Tannice Goddard
Printer: Transcontinental

These stories are works of fiction except for "Country of Evil" which was a finalist in the
Western Canada Magazine Awards in 2004. Names, characters, places, and incidents
either are the product of the author's imagination or are used fictitiously.
Any resemblance to actual persons, living or dead, is coincidental.

CORMORANT BOOKS INC.
215 SPADINA AVENUE, STUDIO 230, TORONTO, ON CANADA M5T 2C7
www.cormorantbooks.com

 Mixed Sources
Product group from well-managed
forests, controlled sources and
recycled wood or fiber
www.fsc.org Cert no. SW-COC-000952
© 1996 Forest Stewardship Council
FSC

Dedicated to the memory of
"our captain" ex-Yeoman Peter Platt, R.N.

CONTENTS

COUNTRY OF EVIL

*B*ecause thick fog shrouded England's northeast coast that spring night in 1941, searchlights had failed to pick out the German bomber until the very last minute. Even as the air raid siren's banshee wail ripped apart the night silence, we recognized the distinctive whoo-whoo-whoo-whoo that was the menacing growl of an enemy aircraft separated from its squadron. As with everywhere else in the United Kingdom, our small Victorian seaside resort of Whitley Bay, Northumberland, had been blacked out for the night. My brother Ted, aged nine, sister Cynthia, aged five, plus myself, aged seven, were preparing for bed. Lengths of black cotton material, distributed by the government and dubbed "blackouts," were drawn across every window of our corner second-floor apartment at 118 Cambridge Avenue, ensuring that no chink of light would escape and attract enemy attention. Our town was only four miles north of the Tyne, a major river that on moonlit nights metamorphosed into a treacherous silver finger pointing unerringly to the locations of the great shipyards that serviced the warships of the Royal Navy. On such nights the Tyneside communities of South Shields, North Shields, Gateshead and Newcastle received the full fury of German attacks. When bad weather thwarted the enemy, however, Whitley Bay often got the bombs meant for our bigger, more industrialized neighbours.

"Under the bed!" Mam ordered, which was what you had to do when there was no time to reach the corrugated iron air raid shelter constructed in the back yard. We children dived under the double bed I shared with my sister, not stopping to switch off the light, and Mam scrambled in beside us. Yanking at the bedclothes, she pulled them down until only a sliver of light showed between the blankets and the floor.

"Why would the Germans want to kill us when we hadn't done anything bad, and they didn't know us and we didn't know them?" Children had asked their mothers in an attempt to puzzle it out. The answer was always: "Germans are evil. Germany is an evil country. That was why, Prime Minister Winston Churchill's gravelly voice announced on BBC radio, "Our brave lads are fighting at the Front."

The Front wasn't a country but lots of countries, and if "our lads" wouldn't fight they were put in prison, and if they ran away from a battle they were shot by their own lads, which, the grown-ups assured us, was good riddance to bad rubbish. Mr. Churchill had also told our mothers to "keep the home fires burning" by knitting balaclavas, scarves and gloves in khaki or navy blue wool every minute they could spare, so that our brave lads wouldn't catch cold while they were fighting the evil Germans. Now we lay on our stomachs, listening as the evil German pilot and his aircraft throbbed above us, and the big guns that protected the coast began booming.

Then we heard a sound we had never heard before. Something metallic was clanking as it travelled over the rooftops of our street and the neighbouring street of Oxford Avenue: a mournful, lonely sound, like an iron bird calling for company.

Mam whispered, "Oh my God!" Huddled against her, we waited.

The world blew up. Blankets lashed our faces at the same instant that a monster crashed through the window and careened around the walls, flinging a chair to one side and hurling shards of glass and pieces of ceiling under the blanket barricade. The closed bedroom door flew open and slammed back against the wall as if kicked by a giant foot. Roof slates sang high over the rooftops before crashing into the street.

Then came a great stillness and a strong, strange smell like burning matches. All I felt was an enormous surprise. Through the ringing in my ears I heard Mam whisper, "The light's still on."

For a while we lay paralyzed; then screams began breaking out up and down the street. A woman's voice was yowling, "Oh Jesus! Oh Jesus! Jesus! Jesus!" Carefully, Mam lifted the blankets and put her head out. We did the same.

We didn't have a window any more. The drapes had disappeared, sucked out into the night, leaving a glaring oblong that invited the German pilot to return and finish us off. Nor did we have a proper ceiling, only part of one. There was no flowered wallpaper left, only paper ribbons that had peeled from the walls and now lay tangled like heaps of discarded Christmas streamers over the skirting boards and the broken bedroom chair. In the centre of the carpet lay the bright green head of somebody's parrot, black eyes staring, beak open to reveal a narrow tongue whitened with plaster dust.

Swear words that we had never heard Mam use began spewing from her mouth, including "Filthy sodden fucking German piece of shit!" and "Oh Christ, some poor buggers have had it!" and "Shit, I've forgotten the gas masks!" Moving inch by inch in case the floor gave way, she wormed out from under the bed, picked up the parrot's head and hurled it through the hole that had been our window. She then reached up and switched off the light, plunging the room into a safe darkness. She began scrabbling in the cupboard where she kept the gas-mask boxes that the government said everyone had to carry with them at all times, then crawled back under the bed and told us to put on our masks. The smell of burned matches was growing strong. Beyond our windowless window fog was reflecting a distant crimson glow that danced like the northern lights, meaning that somewhere near the seafront a house or perhaps several houses were on fire.

My astonishment that somebody who didn't know us would bomb our apartment was so total, so overwhelming, that there was no room for fear. Equally astonishing was the knowledge that complete strangers, who lived in foreign cities that you had never visited and who didn't even speak English, would try to kill you, your family, friends and neighbours, even your pets, with poison gas. What had we done? What had our pets done? The world became dreamlike, as if my family and I were taking part in a movie. We struggled into our masks, pulling the coarse canvas straps back over our heads. As always, a strap caught my long hair and yanked painfully at my scalp, so I pulled my mask off again. Their novelty had worn off long ago; now we children despised them even though they were gifts from the government and the grown-ups told us they had cost a lot of money. We were jealous of our baby cousin Paddy who was too tiny for a mask and needed to wear Aunty Liz's wetted handkerchief across his face, and we were indignant that our cousin Peter, aged four, was the proud owner of a pink and blue Mickey Mouse gas mask. It didn't seem fair that little kids could have a fun mask and babies only needed to wear a handkerchief, while we bigger kids had to struggle for breath within a smelly black rubber bag with a pig-like snout and goggly frog eyes that always fogged up. I began grumbling, but Mam, who was usually a smiley person, lost her temper, yanked off her mask and yelled at me "to put that bloody thing on!" Reluctantly, I dipped my face into the mask and tightened the straps while she did the same to hers. Then we all lay slowly cooking within the smelly rubber and listening to the flapping noises the rubber made against our cheeks as we breathed.

The screaming and weeping in the street were increasing. In the distance rose the fainter screams of people living in Oxford Avenue. Most of the screams came from women and children because of all the brave lads fighting at the Front. For perhaps ten minutes we remained under the bed, not grumbling too much because the mask made our voices sound distant and echoing, as if lost at the back of a big cave. Talking also made the frog eyes steam up. Slowly, the interior of our masks grew wet with condensation. Then the high, steady note of the All-Clear siren climbed the night, indicating that the German bomber had gone away. Ripping off the gas masks, we gasped for air.

The first thing Mam did was to sling a blanket over the

curtain rod to make a blackout curtain. She told us to keep our clothes and shoes on in case the evil German pilot returned, then made us sit on the bed with our backs against the headboard and our shoes dirtying the bedcover. She took out the air-raid box (another thing the government said every family had to have), which contained gauze bandages, adhesive bandages, cotton batting, scissors, aspirins, a bottle of iodine, a bottle of cough mixture, a packet of digestive biscuits and a big bottle of water. She gave each of us a drink of water and two digestive biscuits. She told Ted and me that we didn't have to go to school in the morning because she didn't know if Rockcliffe School was still standing. My brother and sister and I fell asleep, warmly tangled together like a heap of puppies.

Next morning, a team of older men in coveralls and tin hats examined our apartment ... older men because of all the young men having to fight at the Front. As with other apartments in Cambridge Avenue, ours was repairable, which was just as well because many months of bombing had reduced the supply of rental housing to zero. After the men had gone Mam told us to put on our coats, then helped us fix the long straps of our gas mask boxes across our chests so that the sharp corners of the box didn't cut into our hips. Thus armed against poison gas, we joined the groups of people picking their way through the bricks and slates and broken glass that littered Cambridge Avenue and Oxford Avenue. The pig bins that the government had placed at the street corners, and that were emptied once a week, had been blown apart. The apple cores and vegetable peelings carefully saved by our mothers for the pigs (as part of our mothers' efforts to keep the home fires burning) were smeared all over the road.

Older workmen and women wearing men's coveralls were knocking shards of glass out of shattered windows, pushing great brooms about the sidewalks and roads and dumping debris into handcarts. This was another shocking thing: in order to keep the home fires burning and free young men for the Front, the government had given unmarried women the choice of either joining His Majesty's forces or performing men's jobs such as driving tractors and double-decker buses and riveting and welding in the armaments factories. It mixed our minds up because the school picture books showed only ladies in dresses who baked and washed the dishes and looked after children. Never did the picture books show ladies using a welding gun or driving a double-decker bus, and never ever did ladies wear men's coveralls. It was one of the street-cleaning ladies who told Mam that the strange iron voice we'd heard calling overhead was not a bomb. It was, she said, a land mine, which was many times more destructive.

The mine had landed in the middle of several small streets of Victorian row housing built at right angles between Oxford Avenue and the bed-and-breakfasts lining the wide seafront road known as The Promenade. As we approached, we saw air raid wardens and policemen keeping sightseers and would-be scavengers at bay behind a rope barricade while workmen dug for bodies. We knew this area well because Mam used this route to walk my brother and me to Rockcliffe School. Every school day we had passed housewives, aprons around their waists, turbaned heads lumpy with iron-toothed curlers, getting an early start on the housework. Rinsed milk bottles glistened in neat rows on spotless white-stone front steps, waiting for the milkman with his horse and cart; sparkling windows reflected the passersby;

7

polished brass letterboxes and door-knockers defied anyone to desecrate their gleam with sticky fingers. Sometimes a housewife had frowned at us from behind white or cream lace curtains, ready to bang on the window if we dared to try and sneak a flower from her pretty little front garden. Now there were no gardens. There were no houses. There were no housewives. In their place was a vast, deep hole out of which piles of bricks and plaster, roof slates, ripped books, bits of carpet, shoes, tangled clothes and parts of suitcases towered like a frozen whirlpool.

We never learned the toll of dead and injured because the government would not disclose numbers in case the Germans used them for propaganda. Housing inspectors declared that while Oxford Avenue was badly damaged, most of it was repairable. The bed-and-breakfasts of The Promenade, however, were in ruins, the beams supporting the slateless roofs angled like blackened bones against the sky, the shattered windows staring blindly at the North Sea, too damaged to host anything now but cats left ownerless by the land mine, and rats. The houses still standing at the southern end of the land-mine site were also declared uninhabitable. For three weeks workmen shoveled rubble to make a road wide enough for trucks to enter and retrieve salvageable items for distribution at a community centre. They erected signs stating DANGER. KEEP OUT. TRESPASSERS WILL BE PROSECUTED. Then they left.

Before this, evil had been something that slid through our minds like jellyfish — slippery and shapeless. With the land mine, we children knew at last what evil was, and its essence was German.

Now, instead of Mam walking Ted and me to Rockcliffe School via Oxford Avenue and the little streets, we had to use Whitley

Road, the main shopping area, which doubled the length of the walk. One morning, Ted and Cynthia came down with the flu, and Mam was unable to find a babysitter. "You'll have to walk to school by yourself today," she told me. "You're seven years old now, so you know better than to go near the bombed area, right? And you know better than to pick up anything that looks like a pen or a lost parcel, right? Remember it's not a pen or a parcel, it's a booby trap those evil Germans use to try and blow up little English boys and girls. If you see something like that, remember where it is, then tell a teacher as soon as you get to school and they'll tell the police. Be a good girl, use Whitley Road and you'll be fine. No talking to strangers, just go straight to school. Don't forget your gas mask." She stood at the door and waved me goodbye until I turned the corner.

The morning was clear and sunny, but an icy wind careening off the North Sea was cutting through my clothes and stinging my nostrils with salt. Within minutes I was shivering with cold. Making sure no grown-up was watching, I dodged toward the bombed area, knowing that this route would shorten the walk to school by twenty minutes.

At the edge of the wasteland that used to be the little streets, I paused. Nearby, the sign reminded me TRESPASSERS WILL BE PROSECUTED. I peered at the ruined houses edging the site, alert for workmen who would order me to go back and use Whitley Road. There were none. The only sound was the wind moaning through the ruins of the bed-and-breakfasts. I began hurrying along the rough road carved between the mounds of broken glass, bricks and slate, my shoes pattering over the gritty debris left by the trucks. Soon, the habitable part of Oxford Avenue lay

9

far behind me. On my left lay the ruins of the concreted backyards of the once-busy bed-and-breakfasts, their walls standing like grave markers between the sea and me. To my right lay the most badly damaged part of Oxford Avenue, its houses empty while awaiting repairs. In front of me stood the street of still-standing but uninhabitable houses. Rockcliffe School lay two or three streets beyond.

I had reached the halfway point when a man wearing a brown suit walked slowly out of one of the uninhabitable houses and stood very still, staring at me. I knew from the grown-ups that if you saw a man wearing a suit, not a uniform, it meant he held an important civilian job and didn't have to fight at the Front. For maybe a minute the man remained immobile, staring as I continued hurrying along the road. Then his head moved in a slow arc as his gaze searched every part of the deserted site. He stared again at me. Slowly and steadily, he began walking towards me, never taking his gaze from my face.

Instinct stilled my feet. The only sounds were the whining of the wind and the faint rattle of the stranger's shoes on the littered road. So total was the surrounding emptiness that it seemed as if he and I were the only creatures left alive in the world. Then came something that perhaps only young children can experience, for, like wild animals, they still live close to the earth. As the man walked slowly and deliberately toward me, I saw that many thick, black rods, like spears, had begun growing out of his head. The spears continued growing and multiplying, reaching far into the air above him and pointing far below his shoulders. When they stopped growing the man wore a huge black halo. The darkness cast by this halo was so intense it turned his clothes black.

Everything within me told me I had to get away.

The door to the concreted backyard of a nearby bed-and-breakfast had been blown off. My feet came to life. I scrambled over mounds of rubble, the corners of the gas-mask case banging painfully on my hip, then ran through the empty doorway and over the broken bricks and shattered glass of the backyard. Another broken doorway led into what had once been a kitchen, its lead pipes now angled over a smashed sink. The bitter odours of cat urine and damp were overwhelming. A passage led to the closed front door. I ran to open the door, planning to escape along The Promenade and thus reach Rockcliffe School via the seafront. To my dismay, the door was bolted at the top, far out of my reach. The front room was to my right, its splintered door slumping from one hinge. Glass exploded under my shoes as I ran inside and toward the shattered bay window, planning to climb out and escape that way. However, when I reached the window I saw that this house was the kind whose front steps arched over a basement courtyard before they met the sidewalk. The steps had been blown away, and now a wide gap and a huge drop lay between me and safety. There was no way I could make such a leap without falling into the courtyard and breaking my legs.

Panicking, I dodged back into the passage. Where to hide? I ran towards the small dark cupboard under the stairs, thought about black beetles and changed my mind. I ran into the back room. The door was blown off, the window glass blown out and the wallpaper hung in swathes. Shards of glass, broken wooden slats and ceiling plaster littered the floor. Someone had defecated in a corner. In the aperture between the fireplace and the window stood a wrecked wardrobe, its partly-open doors revealing a dried-up shoe. I ran towards it, planning to climb inside and close the doors, then noticed a very narrow gap between the wardrobe and the wall behind it. Turning, I forced my body backward deep into the gap. Then I waited.

Came the steady crunching of glass in the backyard. My heart swelled and air snorted through my nose. I stopped breathing through my nose and began pulling in air through my mouth.

Footsteps crunched through the kitchen. Slowly, the man walked into the passage and halted outside the back room.

Silence.

The footsteps crunched toward the wardrobe and halted. I breathed through my mouth. The wardrobe rocked as the man pulled the doors wide open. I stopped breathing altogether.

Silence.

The footsteps crunched slowly back into the passage and toward the front room. I breathed through my mouth. Glass spat over the floor as he moved to the bay window. Another pause and I knew that he knew that not even a grown-up could make that leap. The footsteps moved slowly back to the passage and halted. The front door rattled as he unbolted it. Silence. He was checking to see if I'd somehow managed to reach The Promenade. The door closed. A few more steady footsteps, then a door scraped open. The cupboard under the stairs. I heard him grunting as he went down on his knees and crawled inside. Patting noises told me he was feeling around the floor. A pause, then he backed out. The door clicked shut. Slowly, steadily, his footsteps crunched up the stairs. Each stair tread creaked. His footsteps trod a circle in the bedroom above my head. Another faint sound indicated that he had opened the door of a closet.

A pause, then a soft thud as the door closed. The footsteps moved toward the front bedrooms. He walked around a big front bedroom. Then a smaller bedroom. Another pause, then the footsteps returned to the top of the stairs. Once again came the slow, steady creak of each stair tread. The footsteps crunched along the passage and halted outside the back room.

A strange calm and a distancing came over me. If he found the space and pulled me out, I don't think I would have felt a thing.

"Little girl, I know you're in here!" His voice echoed through the ruined rooms. His tone was kindly and what we working-class children called "posh."

I breathed through my mouth.

"Little girl, I've found your pretty red hair ribbon, so I know you're here. Please come out and let me give it to you. If you don't come out I'll have to keep it. Don't you want your pretty red hair ribbon?"

Something swelled in my throat, forcing me to swallow. The sound was like thunder.

"Little girl, I'm a good friend of your mummy's. She knows you're here and she's asked me to fetch you home. She's terribly worried about you. Please don't worry your poor mummy. Please come out."

How had he known that? Then Mam must have sent him, after all! I was about to step forward when I remembered the black spears and knew I must not move.

Slowly, the man walked into the room and crunched toward the window. A hand with nicely manicured nails and wearing a gold wedding ring rested on the broken window sash. He was less than three feet away. The cold wind lifting around the room carried a faint scent toward me: Imperial Leather, the good soap and aftershave lotion that Mam had given Uncle Billy on his birthday. A brown left shoe and part of a brown trouser leg appeared. The shoe was polished and had fancy tooling over the instep. The trouser leg had a neatly pressed cuff.

If the man turned to the left he would see me. Such a terror came then that my body seemed to dissolve and another me stepped backwards, out of my body and into the safety of the wall behind me. I could hear my blood roaring.

He turned to the right and crunched toward the fireplace. I heard grunting noises and the sound of a wooden slat being rattled up the chimney. The noises ceased. Slowly, he returned to the passage then walked into the front room. The slat rattled up the chimney. The rattling ceased and he returned to the passage. Once again he climbed the stairs and walked through the bedrooms. The slat rattled up the chimney of each small fire-place. Slowly, he returned to the landing and descended the stairs. He walked along the passage and into the kitchen. His shoes cracked the glass in the back yard. Then came silence.

For an age I remained hidden behind the wardrobe while the wind whined through the broken window and my legs and panties turned to ice. I had peed myself.

At last I felt that the man had gone away for good. Taking minutes between each step, my ears honed for the slightest sound, I edged out of my hiding place, crept through the back room and kitchen and into the ruined backyard. My eyes were starting out of my head as I strained to see if he were hiding somewhere.

Then I flew back to Oxford Street and went to Rockcliffe School via Whitley Road.

Miss Blackwell was young and without the bad temper that racked so many of the older teachers. Those teachers kept a cane on top of their desks and beat the children on their hands for the slightest infraction of school rules, especially if BBC radio reported bad news of the war. All the same, I feared Miss Blackwell might cane me for having disobeyed the KEEP OUT sign and so I didn't tell her about the man. Instead, I pretended I had been sick. I didn't tell my mother either, in case my disobedience made her angry. However, several times during the next few days Mam wondered aloud if I'd caught the same flu germ as my sister and brother because I had gone "unusually quiet."

The quiet came from having a huge problem to solve. The grown-ups had told us children that Germany was an evil country and that all Germans were evil, which by deduction meant that England was a good country and that all English people were good. Yet the man who had hunted for me through the ruined bed-and-breakfast had been English, and I had known with every pore in my body that he was an evil man. It was the beginning of knowledge that evil is a country in-and-of-itself, coming to rest wherever it recognizes its own.

WALKING ON WATER

"*E*r ..." mumbled Noel Thompson, the new pastor. His ears were bright red. "As a matter of fact, Lucy, we thought we'd give someone else the chance to do the solo this Easter."

Lucy Gustavson thought she must be hearing things. She had been the lead soprano at St. David's for four decades. "But Noel, I've always sung 'I Know That My Redeemer Liveth!'" Her voice rose in anguish. "And this time it'll be in front of the Queen!"

"Ian and I thought we'd have a little change this year," Noel said. He added hastily, "But you're a lucky, lucky girl! We're reserving a seat for you as close to Her Majesty as possible." He thrust towards her a printed card with a pin on the back and a picture of St. David's plus his signature on the front. "Security will be extremely tight," he said, avoiding her gaze. "Glue a recent photo of yourself on the front here, then the undercover agents will let you into the church as quick as a wink! Your name will be first on their list!"

Lucy's stunned gaze sought the choirmaster, who had taken up his post around the same time as Pastor Thompson. Ian Duckett continued stacking hymn books, paying fanatical attention to ensuring that each book lined up perfectly with the one below, but she could tell from his peculiar pose — legs braced, ginger head cocked with one ear turned towards her like a skittery deer checking for danger — that he knew about her exclusion. Too choked up to speak, she left the church.

Her husband Harry's solution was to punch the noses of Pastor Thompson and Choirmaster Duckett out through the backs of their heads. Lucy could only pat him on the shoulder and shake her head. Later, she got out the familiar musical score. It was like a hieroglyph for a beautiful language — not of the tongue, but of the soul. She couldn't believe she had been excluded from singing this soul language before the Queen.

"Face it, none of us are getting any younger, are we dear?" purred local gossip Babs Benson in the produce aisle of Smith's Supermarket. "You're not the only one who can't hit the high notes any more."

In spite of her varicose veins, Lucy had always been a zippy soul who never walked if she could run. Now, with Babs's words clanking in her ears, it took her three times as long to do the housework. In the bedroom, she examined herself in the full-length mirror. At three years she had felt eighteen, at thirteen she'd felt eighteen, at forty-three she'd felt eighteen. Now that she was seventy-three, she still felt eighteen. But why kid herself!

Squinting back at her was a stooped old lady with thick glasses, grey hair and legs mummified in elastic bandages. Taking a deep breath, she reached for high C. The note sounded as true as a silver bell ... well, she thought, for she liked to be honest, perhaps a somewhat cracked silver bell.

Her spirits sank even lower after she'd attached the little photograph to the card. The glum, grey-haired Neanderthal staring back at her did nothing to raise her self-esteem. On the contrary, it sent it plunging.

She assured a bewildered Harry that she no longer wished to sing and told herself she meant it. However, when she found a big potato with a little potato growing out of it and stuck four toothpicks in the bigger potato for legs and two half-toothpicks in the smaller potato for horns and gave it to little Brendan next door, he stared at her.

"What's the matter, Mrs. Gustavson?"

"What do you mean, sweetie?"

"You used to be smiley."

After Brendan had gone, she wept with her face jammed into her pillow so that Harry wouldn't hear her.

As the frenzied preparations for the Queen's visit mounted, so did her misery. Singing had been her only talent; now, she felt she had nothing to offer her community, nothing to offer her Lord. When her best friend Alma caught her in an extra-depressed mood, she advised Lucy to find a substitute.

"What kind of substitute?"

"How should I know? Belly dancing! Stock market! Use your imagination!"

"Oh, very well, Madam Know-It-All. I'll walk on water."

It was a whole week before she and Alma spoke to each other again.

The day of the royal visit crept closer. Red, white and blue bunting decorated the streetlights of the small town; in the High Street, green plants appeared in areas where previously only beer cans and cigarette stubs had flourished. Many businesses painted their storefronts for the first time in years. Strange men in dark suits arrived; they stood staring at rooftops and asking that garbage containers be moved. And in order to prove to the royal visitor that Canada was a melting pot that welcomed recent immigrants, Mayor Smith chose a young girl of Chinese heritage to present a bouquet to the Queen. The girl's family had lived in British Columbia for over 120 years, ten times as long as the family of the mayor.

On Easter Sunday Lucy slept in, worn out by her emotions. As she hurled herself into the bathroom, Harry stood at the bedroom window, his grumbling audible through the quickest shower she'd ever had. "See?" he called above the unaccustomed noise of traffic. "One million Yanks and ten million Canadians, all come to see you and the Queen walk on water."

"Oh, do stop being such an old grump, Harry!"

After she'd raced into her underwear, she peeped through the bedroom drapes and saw that their normally quiet road was a sea of vehicles. Both sidewalks were full of men and women in well-brushed suits and new hats heading towards Saint David's. "Oh, I do hope they've kept my seat behind the Queen!" she gasped, throwing on a new dress in brown linen. Then she slashed her lips with orange lipstick and jammed on her head a new blue-feathered hat which was a copy of the hat worn by the Queen to Ascot. Harry limped after her, anxious to help and grumbling all the way.

"Stupid fuss. Why don't you address the Queen as Your Royal Lowness? That way she'll remember you."

"Oh, do stop being such an old grump, Harry!"

"She gets constipation and wind just the same as you —"

"But it's royal constipation and wind!"

In the front garden, he serpentined around Snow White and the Seven Dwarfs, hammered on the roof of a Rolls Royce in order to convince its driver not to park in their driveway and as she backed the car out, he shouted, "Mind these crowds! Be back by noon!"

The whole world, it seemed, was visiting their town. People were using their elbows to gain another precious inch; they avoided others' eyes as if friendliness were a weakness that would see the promised royal treat going to others, with nothing left for oneself. Vehicles were parked every which way, even on the sidewalks. When she attempted to turn down the side street leading to St. David's, her progress was blocked by a massive car beside which loomed an equally massive police sergeant. While not impolite, he was not smiling as his gaze searched her lapel.

"Sorry, Ma'am, only those with ID are allowed past this point."

Only then did Lucy realize that she'd forgotten to pin on her identification card. "Oh no!" she cried. "I've left the card on my dresser! My name's on the list! Please let me pass!"

"That's what everybody says, Ma'am. You can find parking in Brewster's Field."

"Oh please believe me, Officer, I've worshipped here for sixty years! Pastor Thompson is keeping my seat! Please, please let me in!"

"The last ten people said the same thing. Sorry, Ma'am. Move on, please."

There was nothing for it but to continue inching forward. Furious with herself for forgetting her ID, terrified by the surging crowds, Lucy inched towards Brewster's Field. And then the police were waving her past the field, where acres of car roofs were packed as close as sardines in a can. She was forced to keep crawling forward. Desperate to remain within reasonable distance of the church, drivers had triple and quadruple parked.

The road led past another field whose entrance was blocked by a big wooden sign warning PRIVATE, KEEP OUT. Inspiration struck. Wasn't this the field that bordered the road that led through the wood that skirted the side road that ended in the paddock where Mel Stewart's house had a driveway big enough for six trucks?

Until that second, Lucy had always considered herself law-abiding. And not particularly strong. Now, she raced from the Honda, lifted the sign as if it were made of paper, hurled it to one side and drove into the field. Other drivers poured in after her, so ecstatic at this sudden miracle of plenteous parking that they didn't notice Lucy careening out of sight.

After ten minutes of breaking the speed limit down various side roads, the scenery grew unfamiliar. She found herself hair-pinning up a mountain. There were no signposts. Horrified, she realised that she was trespassing on a private logging road. Worse, the road had narrowed so much she couldn't turn around.

Grimly, she drove on, searching frantically for a place where she could turn. The road's gravel surface became slip-sliding earth. Concrete blocks appeared on her left, offering minuscule protection from a drop so dizzying that her stomach melted away. And then a black SUV zoomed up behind her.

She drove as quickly as she dared, stones machine-gunning the Honda's underside, the SUV tailgating her. The road shrank to a narrow ledge tacked to the side of an endless cliff; there were no pullouts, only an endless wall of rock. Keeping close to the rocky wall, she willed herself not to look at the chasm only a few feet to her left and prayed that no oncoming vehicle would appear. Suddenly, she saw an opening. Almost overturning the Honda, she hauled at the steering wheel and swerved through the gap. Her tormentor roared past. When she switched off, she could hear the SUV's triumphant bellow dying in the distance.

Trembling, she hunched in her seat, attempting to shake off the terror of the last few minutes and presently recovered enough to look around. She was inside an ancient crater. Dumped at one end was a big pile of sand; at the other was a crumbling container of road salt. She glanced at her watch. 10:00 a.m. The church service would be commencing.

Her mouth opened of its own accord and she began cursing at the top of her voice: those unknown blankety-blanks who had taken over her church and stolen the seats of the regular congregation. Phrases boiled from her lips that she had not even known she knew as she described the moral characters of Noel Thompson and Ian Duckett and how wrong she had been to stop her Harry from punching the pair of them to the middle of next week. Next, she took on all those younger people who wrote

23

older people off, as if they themselves would never be old. After that, she took old age apart for robbing her of the only talent she'd ever had ...

A voice was squawking at her from the rocky walls. Surprised, she stopped shouting and was treated to a few seconds of her own echo laying down the law. At the same time she saw her reflection in the rear mirror: orange lips prominent above a brown bodice, dark eyes beady with anger. She looked and sounded exactly like a furious, elderly duck.

A splutter escaped her lips, then another. And suddenly, the whole scenario seemed so ridiculous that she was swept into a giggling fit, laughing until tears ran. Enjoying a good laugh made her feel as if she had spring-cleaned a sad old house. Another thought arrived: was a sense of humour also a talent? A talent more important in the long run, perhaps, than a fine singing voice? After all, a voice came from the flesh and therefore had to die with the flesh, but a sense of humour came from the spirit ... and the spirit was eternal.

The thought was immensely comforting. And now, she must return home because Harry would be worrying.

As she switched on the engine she noticed a series of ledges stepping up to the sky at the crater's far end. Suddenly curious about the view, she switched off, struggled out of the Honda and began climbing the ledges, passing a few dandelions, grasses, and a small pine tree. When she reached the top ledge, she dropped to her knees, clinging for dear life to the rock.

She gazed down a precipice that plunged for hundreds of feet before it disappeared into a steep downward rush of Douglas firs and hemlocks. All about her, mountains blue with distance rose and fell like a vast ocean stilled in time and silence. Far below, a lake gleamed like a calm sapphire eye. A wind scented with pine was tugging at her hat; only the wind's low singing broke the silence. She could have been the only human being on earth.

Gradually her fear subsided and she began to appreciate the view. Cloud reflections sailed over the lake's surface and disappeared into its far shore. Birds flew across it and, under the water, mountains met each other. Had her vision been sharp enough, she would have seen that she, too, was held within that calm.

As the wind strengthened, it darkened the water like footprints. Minutes passed and suddenly joy opened within her, and the next minute she was on her feet, holding out her arms as if towards a partner. Something flew from her: the feathered hat, somersaulting out of sight like an imitation bluebird. She began singing the "Hallelujah Chorus." Maybe she hit the high notes, maybe she didn't; it wasn't important. Weeds and grasses and dandelions bowed in the wind; the wind sang through the branches of the little pine tree, and its branches, too, were dancing. Above her danced dazzling heights of sky. She was singing full-throated now, reaching for one triumphant note before soaring to another, her voice echoing into the distances so that it seemed as if the very mountains had lifted their voices in song. She sang her thanks for her belly, with its honourable discolorations caused by bearing three children now grown to fine citizens; for her varicose veins, caused by years of serving the public from behind a department store counter; for her age-spotted hands and the good work they had done for her family and for her community; for her voice, that over the years had given great pleasure to herself and to others. She sang for Harry, who was a good husband and for his arthritic hands and hips, caused by years of toiling in water-logged mines. She sang for the fear in his eyes, which was because one of them would have to go first and he couldn't protect her from that, and above all she sang her conviction that one day their spirits would be joined together for all eternity in a holy place of love.

Peace was gentle within her as she drove home. Endless lines of traffic moved past as visitors started on their own long return journeys. She wished her peace on them, for she could see their faces: tired, depressed that they had driven many miles and waited many hours for a glimpse of something that might bring a little glamour into their lives. Now it was all over and they didn't know when another glimpse of a different, ostensibly richer world would come their way. She thought: What a drag it must be for the Queen to have to be protected by bodyguards around the clock.

When finally she pulled into their driveway, Harry hobbled towards her, eyes blazing, his face ashen. He didn't even notice that she had lost her hat.

"Do you realise it's three-twenty, Lucille Gustavson, and I've been searching for you since twelve? I've been phoning everywhere!"

"Sorry I'm late, sweetie-pie. I forgot my ID and they wouldn't let me into the church."

"So why didn't you come straight back? Where've you been, eh?"

She thought about the lake, the clouds and the birds, and herself moving joyfully with them. She said, "I've been walking on water."

"Oh yes, it's all right for some, isn't it, deciding it's all a big joke! I've been sitting by that window —"

"Oh, do stop being such an old grump, Harry! Let's have a nice cup of tea and I'll tell you all about it."

She took his hand, feeling the terror that she had been hurt still trembling within his fingers and led him towards the kitchen.

BIG GIRL

"Betsy's a big girl, isn't she?"

My fork with its burden of mashed potatoes froze in mid-air. For some weeks now Aunty Liz had been picking on me. She was a Marilyn Monroe look-alike and that evening had chosen to wear a copy of the famous white dress from The Seven Year Itch at the goodbye supper my parents were giving for Uncle Pete. He'd been transferred to Mexico for six months. Aunty Liz was staying behind. Smiling into the puzzled faces around the dining table, she leaned back in her chair, a movement that led to her breasts cresting like the prows of a pair of ocean-going liners. "Must run in the family!" she cooed.

This was the "Fabulous Fifties," heyday of the voluptuous Jayne Mansfield, Anita Ekberg, and, above all, Marilyn Monroe. Perhaps "Fleshy Fifties" would have been a more accurate epithet. It was also the era when sexual ignorance was considered "innocence."

Blood burned my cheeks as our dinner guests' gazes fastened on the painful swellings I'd tried to hide under a big sweater. Father Kelly frowned, and RCMP Sergeant Thompson raised his eyebrows at Mrs. Thompson. Bobby Thompson's cheeks were as fiery as my own, and the fact that he was in my class made matters worse. Our guests, however, were kind. Only Uncle Pete and Uncle John laughed.

"Why are you blushing, Betsy?" Aunty Liz chuckled. "Oh, look, everyone! She's blushing!"

"Cut it out, Liz," Dad murmured. He headed St. Catherine's church board but only because it was his turn to be president. I threw Mom a look that begged oh please shut her up! But Mom would never do anything that might embarrass our guests. She made a shushing movement at me with one hand, as if I were the one making them uncomfortable.

Aunty Liz continued chuckling, and so did Uncle Pete and Uncle John, who weren't my real uncles because Pete was married to my aunt and John was his older brother. Ignoring Mom's "Betsy, where are you going?" I leaped up and ran through the sensuous mist of Chanel No. 5 that hung around my aunt. In the back garden, with a breeze from Georgia Strait cooling my cheeks, I stormed towards a yellow rose bush. There, I tore off every blossom.

"Betsy," Mom's conciliatory voice called, "dessert's ready."

"I don't want any!"

· "Oh, do come and have some dessert, Betsy," Mrs. Thompson cried. The kindness in her voice caused tears to prickle my eyes.

"How about some homemade peach ice cream?" Mom called.
"N-no."

Peach ice cream was my most favourite favourite. I blamed
my parents for my loss and most of all I blamed the "bleached
blonde with the tits." That's how Sergeant Thompson had
described Aunty Liz to Mrs. Thompson, unaware that I was sun-
bathing on the other side of the garden fence. His contemptuous
tone, however, did not match the way his gaze had followed my
aunt when she'd appeared in a tight white sweater and red shorts.
Mrs. Thompson's exasperated voice had responded, "Common
as dirt, that one. She never learns."

"Tits" was a four-letter word. Ian Foster, the class jerk, mouthed
it when no teachers were around, excitement mottling his face
as we girls shrank in our seats and his pals sniggered. My girl-
friends and I did not dare to say "breasts." If forced to refer to
that part of the body we said "bosom," which was the word used
by our mothers and by our hygiene teacher, Miss Tinsley. "Bosom"
did not engender pornographic images of twin mounds of soft
naked flesh; instead, it projected something smooth and solid
such as a plastic foam cushion. I repeated, "The bleached blonde
with the tits, as common as dirt," as I edged to a spot where I
could watch the Marilyn Monroe look-alike forking cake into
her red mouth with its beauty spot inscribed below her left
cheek. She was younger than Mom by six years and was the only
" blonde" adult in the room. My friends and I, nervously picking
our way around the potholes of puberty, had already noticed
that blondes possessed a special power to blow up the world.
Blonde Bombshell. Dynamite Blonde. Blonde TNT. There were
no equivalent phrases for brunettes or redheads. Gentlemen

married brunettes but they preferred blondes. Venus was pagan and blonde; the Virgin Mary, Christian and brunette. All this hinted at a dubious morality on the part of blondes.

And I — although I'd inherited Dad's brown eyes — was as blonde as Aunty Liz.

The would-be Marilyn suddenly rose, jiggled on her white stiletto heels to the open French doors and called, "I'm sorry if I hurt your feelings, Betsy. Please come back."

She'd apologized on other occasions for hurting my feelings, but she still went on hurting them, laughing, saying it was only fun, she hadn't meant anything. Although I knew I should wish Uncle Pete good luck, my feet marched me towards the back door, through the kitchen and up to my bedroom. Mom didn't come after me, didn't arrive with cake and ice cream and sympathy. The sense of double abandonment was agonizing. Until a few weeks ago I'd looked on Aunty Liz as my best friend. Now she wasn't, and Mom wasn't supporting me either.

That's when hatred offered itself as a lifeline. I thought about the previous week, when school broke up for the summer. Uncle Pete was a mining engineer, and Aunty Liz worked at a beauty salon. They had no kids and were quite well off. A month earlier they had sold their first house and bought a bigger house near my school. When my aunt caught sight of me in the school field and crossed the road to say hello, every student stood rooted to the spot, including the two gaping male teachers on duty. Women's magazines warned that blondes should never wear red because it made them look common: my aunt's scarlet wool sweater stretched a second skin over each pointed breast, her stiletto heels made her hips sway like a ship in a gale, and a breeze lifted the hem of her scarlet circular skirt, revealing a white lace petticoat foaming around her shapely legs. When she reached the school she placed both hands on the railings, laughing and tossing her hair. I believe she was well aware of the effect she created and gloried in it. Even if God hadn't made her a Marilyn Monroe look-alike, here was one woman who genuinely rejoiced in being female. After she'd wiggled away, and Ian Foster discovered that she was my aunt, he and his gang made my life hell with their jokes about tits, knockers, milk jugs, boobs, melons, ad nauseam.

"The bleached blonde with the tits, as common as dirt," I repeated to my bedroom walls.

Yet something was stirring in a dark secret place inside of me, like the snake in the Garden of Eden slithering under a stone. Even though I was scared stiff of boys, this other part of me longed to have male heads turn to look after me the way they turned to look after my aunt. I wanted to reduce boys' knees to jelly the way my aunt reduced men to grinning speechlessness. Yet my friends and I were neither supposed to think of boys nor to model ourselves on movie stars; instead, we had to model ourselves on our homemaker mothers. Never had I seen a man's head turn to look after any of them.

Only when the last guest had disappeared did Mom come to see me. A soft rap sounded on my door; her exhausted face appeared and she entered holding a plate of cake and ice cream. The scent of Chanel No. 5 entered the room with her, as if my aunt had infiltrated every corner of the house.

"I saw your light on," she whispered. "You should've said

goodbye to Uncle Pete, you know. You won't see him for six months. He said to give you his love."

"I hate them," I said, not looking at the cake. "I wish Aunty Liz was going with him instead of staying here." Because of the shameful desire to look like my aunt, I spat, "She's so dumb!"

"Crude, yes. Dumb, no," Mom murmured, holding out the plate and a spoon. "Don't forget they bought that house so they could be near us. It's wicked to hate people, Betsy."

"I do so hate them!"

"We're supposed to forgive seventy times seven, you know that," Mom yawned. "Remember those Israelites whose land was destroyed because they followed their will, not God's? Book of Samuel, I think. I always forgive, but I admit it's difficult."

Trying to get Mom to understand how my aunt affected me was like using one's fingernails to dig through a concrete wall. "Tell her she can't come here unless she shuts up about me!" I demanded, lifting the spoon full of peach ice cream.

"How can I do that when she's my sister? When you're grown up you'll understand. She's nearing thirty and I think that bothers her," she said, stroking my arm. "I'll speak to Lizzie, tell her she can't expect you to understand adult humour."

"She never listens to you," I mumbled through a mouthful of cake. I added, without any basis whatsoever, "She thinks you're stupid." I wanted Mom to hate Aunty Liz as much as I did.

Mom's conciliatory expression faded and a parched look took its place. She said stiffly, "Oh, I think Liz has many reasons to listen to me. Anyway, it's as Marg Thompson says, we should be sorry for someone like her."

"For her?"

"Because she'll be all alone for six months and she hasn't got a baby to keep her out ... to keep her company, has she? And I know Pete's asked John to take her out now and then, but a brother isn't the same as a husband." An expression I couldn't fathom darkened her eyes, but all she said after she'd dropped a kiss on my cheek was, "I don't think your father understands how these suppers take it out of me. It's not as if they're potluck. Now clean your teeth and don't forget your prayers."

I didn't say my prayers. Instead, I stared into the darkness. Males, I'd noticed, used their fists as weapons, but females used their tongues, and sometimes the tongue seemed a more destructive weapon than the fist. Aunty Liz tied my own tongue in knots.

My goal became to avoid her as much as possible, which wasn't difficult, because Uncle John did as Uncle Pete asked and often picked her up from the salon and took her to dinner. That was the same month that Bobby's seventeen-year-old sister got married in a rush, a grim-faced Sergeant and Mrs. Thompson driving the teenaged couple to the church themselves, leaving a bewildered Bobby to look after their dog. It's the only time I've seen a bride crying, her navy-clad back (not even a new dress, let alone the traditional white gown) turned like a barricade against the young bridegroom frozen on the seat beside her. Even from our front garden gate I could see the livid crimson of his acne.

"Brian's not a police sergeant for nothing, Chas," I overheard Mom tell Dad that evening as I washed the dishes. They were in the dining room. "You commit the crime, you do the time. That's his philosophy."

"At least Janey didn't try to get rid of it."

"What, and be charged with murder?" Mom exclaimed.

Murder? If you committed murder you got hung by the neck until you were dead. They were talking in the dining room. I strained to hear more.

"Betsy's growing into a big girl herself, Eileen. Have you told her the facts of life yet?"

The facts of life! A nasty taste soured my tongue. The "facts" were to do with sex, and the only available sex facts came from men's magazines, which were stacked on the pharmacy's top shelves, out of the reach of children. Page after page featured grinning women thrusting out naked breasts and bums at the reader, a strategically raised thigh barricading the crotch as if to warn, "This far and no farther." None of the magazines featured naked men. Checkout girls packed women's magazines in with the bread and teabags and eggs, but men's magazines went into separate brown bags, along with disinfectant and mice bait. The message? Men's naked bodies are not entertaining — and women's naked bodies are entertaining and dangerous and dirty.

Dad's question seemed of such vast import to Mom that it was taking her some time to answer. Now she said, "We know learning the facts too soon leads to experimenting. She's only twelve."

"She's nearly thirteen. If you're embarrassed —"

"Liz could do it?" Mom interrupted. "I know you said she's very beautiful but she's not exactly a good example. Is she?"

"I never said beautiful. I said pretty."

"As a matter of fact, I noticed her roots need retouching. I had to smile because it makes her look as if she's wearing a dirty halo. Did you notice that, Chas? A dirty halo?"

"I wasn't looking that closely."

"Oh well, it's not her hairline that men look at, is it? D'you know what Marg told me? She said, 'All that attention since babyhood can really distort one's values, Eileen. Give thanks that you were spared that.' Of course I give thanks I was spared. Were you there when Marg said that?"

"No."

A buffet drawer slammed so violently that a shudder passed through the wall and into the kitchen floor. Who slammed the drawer, I've no idea.

"Fancy buying a four-bedroom house when you've no intention of starting a family!" Mom said. "What I find rather laughable is that it's their second house. We've rented this matchbox for thirteen years."

"Obviously engineers are paid more than assistant store managers. How many times do I have to say I'm sorry, Eileen? Don't keep on, for God's sake."

"I'm not keeping on. I'm saying that I'd like to keep Betsy innocent for as long as possible."

They stopped talking. I finished the dishes, the clashing plates sounding extra loud against the silence emanating from the dining room. My attention had been caught by the word "innocent." That was another loaded word. If I had to be kept innocent, it was further proof that the facts of life were dirty. They had to be, because a month earlier a local bookseller had been charged with "distributing obscene materials" when he'd sold a copy of *Lady Chatterley's Lover*. My dictionary said that obscene meant filthy, repulsive, indecent and loathsome.

In September I began high school, where a crisis blew up immediately. Over the protests of many parents, the Vancouver School Board brought in "Family Health" for Grades 10 to 12. The program was controversial not only because it described conception and touched on abortion, but also because, for the first time, boys and girls were to take sex instruction together. Parents picketed the education offices, carrying signs emblazoned PROTECT CHILDREN'S INNOCENCE AND LET THEM BE CHILDREN. Later, Ian Foster and his gang had a field day with words like "penis" and "vagina" that had been passed on to them by older brothers. Patsy Donkersloot had a sister in Grade 11 and Patsy breathlessly passed on several pieces of information as we congregated in the girls' washroom. One piece in particular had us reeling. None of us dared ask our mothers if it was true that babies were made by men putting their penises inside women's vaginas, or the infinitely worse question — the act impossible to imagine and treacherous even to consider — had Dad done that to her? The image, however, obsessed me. Eventually, a corrosive, deeply shaming curiosity drove me to Mom. I could only approach the subject by circling.

"Mom, the Virgin Mary was pure because she hadn't been married, right?"

"Yes."

Her high flush and cold tone told me she didn't want to discuss it. And the question burning on my tongue was a dreadful one. I wanted to ask, "Then does that mean that all the other married women (meaning every married woman except my mom) are impure?" One look at Mom's face and the question shriveled in my mouth.

It was Ian Foster who educated us about menstruation. Miss Hazlett was late and Donna Reslaw, whom I didn't like, made the mistake of mentioning that she'd brought a note asking to be excused from gym class. Ian snatched it and danced away, shouting out its contents. The note used words we hadn't heard before, and Ian yelled that Donna had the "curse" and now wore "blue packets" just like "the tarts and old bags." As Donna tearfully denied it, he proceeded to describe the curse to his giggling cronies. My friends and I had at some time discovered thick white pads hidden at the backs of drawers, but our mothers had said they were for removing makeup. Stunned, shamed beyond words — Ian made it clear that having the curse was something dirty that happened only to girls — we huddled around Donna in the girls' washroom.

"Mom says it's come very early and it's called menstruation, but vulgar people call it the curse. Now I can have a baby," she wept. Then she added viciously, as if menstruation were an infectious disease and it served us right if we caught it because we hadn't washed our hands properly, "Mom says all girls get it, so you needn't think it won't happen to you, because my mom says it will!"

No matter how desperately I needed information, there was no way I could mention this incident to Mom. But Aunty Liz had somehow got wind of it, for suddenly, there she was, a perfumed vision in skin-tight blue sweater and matching calf-length pants known as pedal-pushers, cornering me in the garden and saying, "You know, Betsy, you're getting to be a really big girl. I heard what happened at school. Has Eileen spoken to you about getting the curse?"

Can't you even use the proper term? I fumed inwardly as heat suffused my face. Mom had been one of those picketing the school board offices. Anguished in case my aunt told me something that Mom didn't want me to hear, I gargled some sort of a reply.

"Because Eileen can ask me to tell you. Such things don't embarrass me because they're perfectly natural. You'll be getting the curse soon enough, earlier than your friends, most likely. You're a big girl ... look how you're developing!" Playfully, she smacked my bum.

It was as if she was announcing that Mother Nature planned to exile me to a frightening foreign country, where my only companion would be the unlikable Donna. My mouth opened and out came, "Keep your hands off me, you ... you old bag!"

Terms like "tarts" and "old bags" were used by Ian Foster to describe the painted women who loitered under the street lamps in the Downtown East Side. I hadn't known that such a shocking phrase had been lying in wait under my tongue, yet there it was, boiling out of my mouth into the freshness of the garden. For a few seconds, she gaped at me while I stood numb with horror. Then she blew up.

"By God, you need to scrub out your mouth! Well, who cares what your nosy neighbours say about my reputation! The hell with the lot of you!"

She stormed into the house and I waited with chattering teeth for my parents to appear, knowing they would punish me severely. And what was this about her reputation? Women with reputations were the women who loitered under the street lamps, and they were the lowest form of life in the whole of Canada because, said Father Kelly, they "dragged men down into sin." He regularly led campaigns to save the women's souls. And the neighbours were saying that my aunt was like those women?

After a few days, it became clear that she hadn't complained to my parents, but there was no peace for me. Instead, the conviction grew that she'd get her own back by suggesting in front of guests that I would soon get the curse. After all, I told myself, fluctuating between misery and horror, she'd deliberately drawn attention to my breasts.

In December, my thirteenth birthday arrived. "Your friends must leave by seven," Mom informed me. "You've got school the next day, and the dining table's needed for a meeting."

Patsy and Ann gave me an English lavender bath set and a craft box of glass beads that could be mixed and matched to make sets of necklaces, bracelets and earrings. I loved these presents: they represented the nice side of growing up, not the threatening side. My parents' present had secretly disappointed me — a jewel box of polished wood — but instead of a pretty ballerina twirling to ballet music when the lid was opened, it offered a little teddy bear circling to "The Teddy Bear's Picnic." The teddy bear didn't match the image that came with my entering the teens. A sophisticated young adult is how I saw myself.

All was going well until Aunty Liz arrived in an ankle-length, sherbet-pink spangled gown that made Mom and her beige shirt-dress fade into oblivion. Diamond earrings sparkled through my aunt's soft blonde hair; she was clutching a big, prettily wrapped box to her cleavage, and from the excited smile she flashed my way, she had forgotten the confrontation in the garden. Uncle John was in evening dress, smiling behind her.

Dad was in the kitchen when Aunty Liz arrived, and when he walked into the living room he burst out, "Whee-wheeoooo!" Although it was immediately clear he wanted the earth to swallow him, I still hated him for wolf-whistling, hated the way my aunt's exposed breasts resembled two ripe golden pears, hated the way my friends were gaping, hated the stricken look in Mom's eyes. Hated, too, the immediate desire that flamed in the secret part of my soul for a dress just like that. The gown was a copy of one worn by Marilyn Monroe in *Some Like It Hot*. When my aunt sat down the skirt parted to reveal her left leg almost up to the panty line. She breathed in her little-girl voice, "Johnny, you go first."

"Would you like a safety pin for that skirt?" Mom cut in. "Where on earth are you going?"

"Panorama Room," Aunty Liz said. "Dinner dance. For God's sake, Eileen, why would I want a safety pin? Go ahead, Johnny."

Dropping a tiny package into my lap, and before I could open it, Uncle John announced, "Chanel for another dynamite blonde!" Mom's disapproval was palpable, but she needn't have worried. Because the treacherous part of me had lusted to look like my aunt, I immediately decided never to allow her trademark perfume to sully my skin.

Aunty Liz was bouncing excitedly in her seat as she handed me her own present, and it was shamefully obvious that she wasn't wearing a brassiere. Reluctantly, I tore off the wrapping and opened the box. As my friends leaned to look and my aunt broke into, "Happy birthday to you," my hands stilled on what looked like a heap of transparent rainbows. I wanted to die. When

I didn't speak, Aunty Liz stopped singing and reached into the box with a breathless, "To celebrate your growing up!" Triumphantly, she held up a transparent scarlet nylon brassiere and matching bikini panties with a tiny gold key attached to the crotch, the kind of lingerie that made Mom snort "Tarty rubbish!" whenever we shopped for our own serviceable white cotton underwear. The grin splitting Dad's face disappeared as Mom's fingers hooked his arm; the expression on her own face would have metamorphosed anyone but my aunt into a pillar of salt, while my friends looked away, embarrassed to view lingerie — particularly that sort of lingerie — in front of the opposite sex. Beneath the scarlet nylon, my aunt's hands looked like fingers of flame. Snatching the lingerie from her, terrified that the colour would have her joking about the curse, I thrust it back into the box and avoided her and Uncle John as best I could. She didn't take the hint. When my friends left and I carried the presents to my bedroom, my aunt wiggled up the stairs behind me. Mom was downstairs, tidying up in preparation for the board meeting.

"Eileen seems to think my present isn't appropriate for you, Betsy, but at the rate you're growing they'll soon fit you, right?" my aunt asked. "I got you four sets. Johnny said not to get you plain white. He thought you'd prefer pretty colours."

That she had dared to discuss the lingerie with him, meaning he'd have imagined it on my body! It would've been bad enough if he'd been my dad, but Uncle John wasn't even my real uncle. Because I couldn't look into her eyes I stared at her false beauty spot and for the first time noticed faint lines, like sparse, finely etched grass, spreading from her upper lip.

43

After a minute she coaxed, "They weren't cheap, you know, I chose the best brand name," as if the lingerie's being expensive would make a difference.

"Oh come on, Betsy," she said at last into my silence, "don't be like Eileen's friends. They're such a bunch of dirty-minded prigs. You need support and I'm surprised Eileen hasn't bought you a bra before this. You're starting to bounce."

Never had Mom mentioned buying me a brassiere. That this bouncer-supreme should do so!

"And the boys like it, you know, you'll attract a lot of attention with a nice shape," she went on, smiling as if she were giving me a fantastic tip. "Come on, Betsy, let's be friends again." Placing her hands a la Monroe on her hips, she turned her left side to me, so that the glittering guided weapons of her breasts threatened my doll collection behind her. "You're going to have my figure, and even though you've got your dad's brown eyes, you're still very much a blonde, just like me." She hesitated, and then added somewhat defiantly, "In fact, I think you look more like me than either your dad or your mom." When I still remained silent, she smiled, "And I'm telling you, Betsy, just like that movie says, Gentlemen ... Prefer ... Blondes." She batted her black mascaraed eyelashes at me in a prodigious wink.

Staring at those fleshy nose cones, I felt that God had betrayed me, first by making me a girl and second by making me look like her, not Mom. Next, she'd be talking about the curse. I got out, "You're not my mom."

My revulsion must have been in every syllable because she jerked back as if I'd hit her. Her smile vanished and a painful crimson flooded under her careful makeup. Flinging herself away from me, she cried, "Oh, for Chrissake, you're a big girl now!"

As she teetered down the stairs, clinging to the handrail in case her silver stiletto-heeled sandals tipped her head first into the hall, I flung the bedroom window open in order to rid my room of the smell of her perfume.

Some thirty minutes later as I was wrestling with my homework in the kitchen, brakes screeched in the road outside. Then the front door banged open and I heard my aunt demand, "Where is she?" Next minute, she was in the kitchen. Behind my aunt were my bewildered parents, and beyond them, the shocked faces of the board members. Storming towards me as fast as her tight gown would allow, and while the other adults gaped, she hurled into my lap a little plastic doll, the kind sold by Woolworth's. A cotton diaper wrapped its pudgy limbs — blue, to indicate it was a boy — a soother filled with water protruded from its mouth and the card dangling from one wrist announced its name was "Baby Wet-Me."

"Play with that, then!" my aunt shrilled, glaring at me. "And stay a baby, little girl!"

My tongue was no longer in knots; it was off at the root. Mom turned an outraged glare on my dad. He only stared at the floor.

Surely Mom would protest, even if Dad didn't? But no, we had guests, and Mom would never embarrass guests. It was Mrs. Thompson who protested as my aunt whirled past her, "Elizabeth, that was uncalled for!" Then my aunt was gone, her perfume tainting the air. We heard Uncle John's station wagon roar and then fade.

Only one thought was with me: my aunt had humiliated me in public yet again and my parents had been as powerless as I to prevent her attack. Turning carefully — I was wearing newly-constructed earrings with a matching necklace — I placed the doll on the kitchen counter and kept my back to it. Blood was roaring in my ears.

"She's your sister," Dad told Mom before suggesting to the embarrassed board members that their meeting should continue. After that, I couldn't concentrate on my homework. Inside I was weeping tears of futility, but there was no way I would allow those tears to spill.

After the guests had left, Mom said tightly, "Chas, I need to talk to you. Please wash the dishes, Betsy, and don't come upstairs."

At one point I heard the crash of breaking china, but in spite of straining my ears — I didn't dare listen outside their door in case they opened it — the only sound was a low, bitter murmur, the way a winter wind moans through the broken windows of a derelict house. When they finally came downstairs, Dad's face was white and the expression in Mom's eyes was so blighted it frightened me. Hoping against hope, I waited to hear them say, "Betsy, we won't allow your aunt to visit us again," but they said nothing. I knew then that whatever it was between them they were trapped too deeply to help me. I was on my own.

Next morning, I slipped into the back garden. I was crying inside, not only for the way things used to be between Aunty Liz and me compared to the way things were now, but also because of the major mortal sin I'd committed during the night. I'd dreamed I was in a public park wearing nothing but the transparent scarlet lingerie, posing before a group of wolf-whistling boys whose hands reached out to touch me. The reaching hands excited me in a way I couldn't begin to name. Waking with a start,

I found myself bathed in sweat, my heart thudding, a pleasurable throbbing between my legs. The memory of what happened next made me ill with shame. Never ever would I confess it to Father Kelly, and that in itself was a major sin. My soul was doomed for all eternity.

Looking miserably about me, I saw how nature was in a constant state of flux: leaves, flowers, insects, birds: everything started off as one shape and ended up as something that bore no resemblance to its beginnings. But nobody sniggered and used dirty words when plants and animals and birds changed and matured. I told myself it was only people who became dirty, particularly females, with "tits" and the "curse," and women who were "bags" and "tarts." It's Aunty Liz's fault, I wept. If she hadn't given me the tarty lingerie, my hands never would have done what they did.

Shortly afterwards, my aunt came down with some sort of germ and for the next little while we saw nothing of her. Nor did she telephone every day, which was unusual for her. At the same time, a house that Mom had always liked came up for rent and my parents broke our lease and prepared to move. Every spare minute was spent packing.

And then Uncle John left so suddenly for Alaska that he didn't visit us to say goodbye.

"She must miss him. After all, they went out a lot together, didn't they?" Mom said lightly to Dad as she wrapped a cup in newspaper. I was at the kitchen counter, sorting cutlery.

"Did they?" Dad said. He was at the other side of the kitchen table, wrapping plates.

"Theatres and dancing and high-class restaurants, oh my, I

can't remember what that kind of life is like," Mom continued in the same casual tone. "Have you noticed how she's always attracted to older men? All my friends have noticed. They think it's common, the way Liz dresses."

"Watch what you say in front of —"

"Nobody would guess that you and Liz are sisters, my friends told me. Thank goodness, Eileen, they said, you are a lady." Carefully, Mom stacked the cup inside a carton. "I mean, that slit dress! It was really amusing, wasn't it? I thought any minute we'd be forced to view her underwear!" A shrill laugh burst from her lips. It made me jump. "Just imagine, Chas," she said, her lips stretching in a smile while her unsmiling gaze searched his face, "if you were married to Liz and she wore that dress to a dinner with your boss. You'd never get promoted."

"There's a sales report I've got to finish," Dad said, throwing down the newspaper. He moved towards the door.

"Don't leave everything to me, Chas!"

"I've always left everything to you," Dad said. The door banged behind him.

"Not everything, Chas! Not everything!" Mom yelled. Catching my surprised stare, she flushed and then called — not as loudly, but still angrily — "I don't have time to fill Lizzie's entertainment gap no matter what I promised my parents. There's too much junk to pack."

Dad's voice traveled through the door. "That's right, there's too much junk."

In the much more bureaucratic 1950s, moving out of the school area almost always meant children had to change schools. I pleaded with my parents to let me finish the term at my old school, and they promised they wouldn't inform the education authorities until after Christmas. My friends were sworn to secrecy and I hoped that Ian Foster wouldn't find out, for he'd rat on me for sure.

"Thirteen years you've been in this house. My, we're going to miss them. Aren't we, Marg?" Mrs. Baxter, our neighbour three houses down remarked to Mrs. Thompson as she sipped her coffee. Mom had invited Mrs. Baxter to drop by even though her denomination was Baptist.

"We certainly will," Mrs. Thompson said. "You've been the perfect neighbour, Eileen. Like Caesar's wife, you're beyond reproach."

"Beyond suspicion," I said automatically (my class was doing Shakespeare) but nobody was listening. Mrs. Baxter stared at me. "My goodness, Betsy," she smiled, "you're starting to look just like your Aunty Liz!"

"Betsy is the image of my mother when Mother was her age," Mom said quickly at the same time as I protested, "But I'm not like Aunty Liz."

"Well, except that Liz's eyes are blue, I'd say you're the living image," Mrs. Baxter said.

"But I'm not like her," I said urgently. "I'm not like her!"

"Betsy's not like Liz at all," Mrs. Thompson snapped. "Liz is a lapsed Catholic."

"Liz didn't marry in church," Mom said, setting down her cup so quickly that coffee splashed into the saucer. "She said if the marriage didn't work it would be easier to divorce. It's only prac- ticing Catholics who are forced to wear a ball and chain until death do you part."

Then Aunty Liz committed the unforgivable. Ever since my thirteenth birthday, my parents would knock and wait until I called, "Come in!" before entering my bedroom. Aunty Liz didn't bother. I didn't even know she was in the house until she appeared in my doorway, mumbling, "Where's Eileen?"

For once, she wasn't made up and her usually carefully arranged hair straggled about her pale face. I was changing out of my school clothes and was stark naked. Her glance went from my breasts (size B already) to my crotch with its sparse bush of pubic hair, and with a wan smile she said, "My, really growing up, aren't we?"

Nobody had seen me naked. Nobody. When my friends and I changed in the gym we politely turned our backs. Aunty Liz would tell Uncle Pete and probably Uncle John too, and from then on, that's how the three of them would see me. They would look straight through my clothes to my swelling breasts and crotch with its sprouting of pubic hair. I couldn't bear it.

Suddenly, she made a strange gurgling sound and stumbled towards the bathroom, leaving me to race into my clothes. When her bloodless face re-appeared, she whispered, "I can't stay. Tell Eileen I need her. Tell her to call me at home."

But I didn't mention her visit. So white-hot was my outrage at her having witnessed my nakedness that I didn't want Mom to have anything to do with her.

Next day, Mr. Hall, our home teacher, distributed permission forms and announced a pre-Christmas treat. A local theatre group was performing Julius Caesar and had offered our school a free matinee for the following afternoon.

"Pay attention to the play because I'll be giving a test on it,"

Mr. Hall said. "And make sure one of your parents signs the permission slip or you'll have to stay behind."

Mid-way through the next morning's class I realized I'd forgotten to have the slip signed. It was impossible for me to forge my parents' signatures, but I knew Mom and Aunty Liz wrote in a similar hand, and Aunty Liz, of course, lived near the school. I didn't want to ask a favor of this woman whom I now loathed, but I was desperate.

At noon I raced down the street of elegant houses, their roofs and windows festooned with Christmas lights. Aunty Liz's house was the only one left undecorated. As was usual the back door was unlocked. Pushing it open, the permission slip in my hand, I cried, "Aunty Liz, it's Betsy. Are you home?"

A bump sounded overhead, as if something had fallen. Up the stairs I ran, becoming aware of a queer, thick smell as I reached the landing. To my surprise, a stained bath towel lay on the carpet ... surprise, because whatever else my aunt was, her housekeeping was spotless. Her bedroom was another shock. The smell here was stronger, and steam wreathed the ceiling, apparently from an electric kettle that had fallen to the floor. Opened packets of herbs littered the bedside table, and stained towels and sheets of newspaper lay alongside the bed. From somewhere among the chaos of bedclothes came the buzzing of a telephone fallen off the hook. My aunt was in bed.

"Are you sick, Aunty Liz?" I began, lifting the kettle and then dropping it because it was red hot. "Shall I open the win ..."

And then I halted, paralyzed. Only the sweat-soaked blonde hair pasted to the pillow was recognizable. For a few incredible seconds I failed to recognize the dark yellow face itself. My aunt looked as if she'd aged one hundred years. Sweat had darkened the front of her frilly blue baby doll pajama top, her beauty spot had smeared towards her chin and huge brown shadows circled her eyes, which looked like those of a dying animal.

"Oh, Aunty Liz!" I cried, shocked momentarily out of my loathing for her. "Oh, what's the matter, oh, what's happened?"

She croaked something — I couldn't make out what — and I began scrabbling among the blankets for the telephone, crying, "I'll phone Dr. Hammond, I'll phone him right now!"

"S-Stop," she moaned, "stop ... stop ..."

I found the telephone, replaced the receiver and gazed at her, too frightened to speak. Staring at me with animal eyes she whispered, "Migraine. W-Water."

I hadn't known she suffered from migraines. And the queer smell was coming from her, a thick sickly-sweet odour that reminded me of the blood-soaked sawdust on the floor of the local butcher shop. Her lips, usually so bright with lipstick, were cracked and bloodless. Her teeth chattered against the glass I held for her. She could only manage one sip before she collapsed against the pillow.

"Please, Aunty Liz, please let me call an ambulance," I begged, for it was clear that she was desperately ill and had to be helped.

"No." Staring feverishly at me, she whispered. "Why ... you here?"

Only then did I remember my errand. I stammered the reason. "Pen. Drawer."

I found the pen, coughing as steam caught at my lungs,

and once again begged her to let me call our doctor. "I f-forbid it," she whispered, sounding almost angry. "Give me ... p-pen." Trembling almost as much as my aunt, trying not to ingest the smell of her, I supported her while she scrawled Mom's name. At one point, she gasped and her back arched as if she'd been stabbed; her whole body convulsed. The violent movement sent me staggering, my shoe clanged against something metallic under the bed and I heard a sloshing sound. Not knowing what I'd done, I lifted the edge of the coverlet and saw an enamel bucket.

My mind blanked out.

"G-got the c-curse," my aunt gasped. The permission form had fallen from her hand. Closing her eyes, she whispered, "Not ... s-see anybody. S-solemn ... p-promise ... solemn ... p-promise ... "

I have no memory of the return journey to school.

"Are you all right, Betsy?" Mr. Hall frowned, accepting permission slips without bothering to check the signatures. "You look so white."

"I'm all right, sir," I managed. My numbed brain was returning to life. Certain pieces of information that Patsy had whispered to us in the girls' washroom were beginning to come together to make a whole.

Mr. Hall forgot me as excited students fired questions at him. "Put on your coats and gloves," he called. "We'll be walking behind the other classes and there's to be no nonsense en route, understand?"

Later, laughing voices and a recording of "Away in a Manger" reached me as I slowly approached our house with its big cross outlined in white lights on the front door. On the roof of the opposite house, a wooden Santa rode a sleigh and held the reins of a team of reindeer.

Our house was redolent with the aroma of hot punch, sausage rolls and mince pies. My parents, the Thompsons, Father Kelly and several members of our church were sitting in front of a log fire in the living room, enjoying their drinks, listening to carols. They were dressed up; even Sergeant Thompson was resplendent in his scarlet RCMP jacket and black jodhpurs, a bottle of ginger ale prominent alongside his glass. Religious Christmas cards sent a message of love and peace from every available surface, and in one corner stood our Christmas tree, a traditional creche beside it. In the manger, minus its soother and blue diaper, lay the little doll that Aunty Liz had used to humiliate me in front of the board members. Mom had said it was a pity to let the doll go to waste.

Catching sight of me, voices cried, "Happy Christmas, Betsy!"

A huge Christmas card dominated the mantelpiece, its poinsettias livid as blood. Noticing my fascinated stare, Father Kelly said, "From your Uncle Peter. Isn't it a shame, Betsy? He's telephoned to say his tour has been extended. Poor Elizabeth must be so disappointed."

I remained silent. Ever since I'd left the theatre, something had been stirring inside me.

Dad said, "You're very quiet, Betsy. How was the play?"

And suddenly, I knew what was being born within me. I stared at the blood-red pointsettias ...

"Betsy, don't be rude in front of guests. Answer Daddy," Mom said.

"Oh — family argument, " Sergeant Thompson said, setting down his glass. "Good time to nip round and wish Liz a merry Christmas."

My mouth opened. "She's very sick."

"How do you know that?" Dad asked sharply. "Have you been there?"

"Lunch time. She's very sick."

"What! Oh dear, I'd better see how she is!" Mom said, standing up. "Chas, would you look after everyone?" Turning to the guests, she added brightly, "Pete and Liz have just bought their second house," and I saw Dad bend down and begin to untie a shoelace. Then she asked, "What's she got, Betsy, the flu?"

I started with a word my aunt had used. "Migraine."

"Liz has a migraine?" Mom exclaimed. "Liz never gets migraines!"

"She's ... thrown up," I said, feeling my way forward.

"Oh dear, a sick migraine?" Mom said. Turning to Dad, she added with a brittle smile, "Too much alcohol, I suppose. That's the usual excuse, isn't it?"

"Like a ride with Marg and me?" asked Sergeant Thompson, standing up.

Mom turned to me. "Betsy, this is very bad of you," she said sharply. "You should've told me your Aunty Liz was ill the minute you came in. I'm surprised at your lack of consideration."

The shock of the unexpected public scolding broke the dam of rage that had been swelling within me for months. Moving to the crèche, I lifted the Baby Jesus and held Him up the way that Father Kelly held up the Host. I had the attention of everyone in the room. "She didn't want me to tell anyone, her bedroom is too messy," I said, turning Baby Jesus as if inspecting Him for flaws. "Newspapers all over the floor, bowls of herbs everywhere, lots of steam ..." I paused, then held the Baby Jesus so that He faced Uncle Pete's Christmas card. I added clearly, "Even a knitting needle in a bucket under the bed."

In the sudden electric silence I could hear my own ragged breathing. Dad's fingers had stilled around the shoelace.

"Knitting needles?" stammered Father Kelly.

"One knitting needle." I replaced Baby Jesus in the manger. "In a bucket. Under the bed."

Some minutes later, Dad, Mom, Father Kelly and Sergeant Thompson drove away in the sergeant's car, leaving Mrs. Thompson with me. I strained to see Mom, because her face when I mentioned the knitting needle had been a mixture of fear and — for a split-second — something so livid it made me catch my breath. However, Sergeant Thompson's Stetson blocked my view. Our other neighbours had already melted away.

Mrs. Thompson sat like a stone. At one point she rose, poured herself a drink, gulped it down and poured herself another before turning to stare at me.

Now that the step had been taken, my mouth was so dry I had to keep swallowing. I closed my eyes. Something unexpected was happening: salt tears were hurting my throat.

A rustling sound made me open my eyes again. Mrs. Thompson was standing beside me, her drink trembling in her hand.

"D'you know who she is, Betsy?" she asked, and I could smell her breath, like overripe fruit.

"Who she is?" I blinked.

"Elizabeth. D'you know who Elizabeth is?"

"You mean Aunty Liz?"

"She was adamem ... adamant ... that you have her name," Mrs. Thompson mumbled. Turning, she carried her drink to the picture window and stood staring up the street. Darkness had closed in. A street light had wiped out the stars and flooded the road with a sulphurous yellow that threw long shadows behind Santa and his reindeer. I remained in my chair, attempting to make sense of what she'd said.

Do you know who Elizabeth is?

She was adamant that you have her name.

Her name ... Liz, short for Elizabeth. My name ... Betsy, short for Elizabeth ...

In the distance rose the banshee wailing of an ambulance, followed immediately by the blare of a police siren. Mrs. Thompson placed her drink on the windowsill and turned towards me.

And when I saw her eyes, I knew.

JOHNNY, I HARDLY KNEW YOU

*L*eaves whirled like lost birds through the rushing pine-scented darkness, and at the far end of the inn's parking lot a discarded can clattered across the concrete and into the narrow road winding over the fell and down towards England. Johnny hesitated beside his truck, turning his back to the wind and listening as the can's lonely stutter faded. The strange restlessness that had been with him all day was with him still, and this wild autumn weather wasn't helping.

Once, Kilnevin had had two public houses. Now there was only the Kilnevin Inn, where many years ago his father had played Mine Host. Johnny pushed the door open on the hot, crowded bar room smelling of fried prawns and beer. Norm and Ruth, the inn's latest owners, were busy behind the new vinyl-fronted bar. The original bar, its oak counter hollowed by the elbows of three centuries of farm folk, had gone to an antique dealer in America.

"Johnny," Ruth called above the din, "message for you."

Blinking in the white glare of the new neon tubes inserted between the ceiling beams, and exchanging the odd greeting with a neighbour, Johnny pushed his way to the front.

"A woman checked in yesterday from Canada," Ruth told him. "Says she used to know you when her name was Marjorie Clark. Ring a bell?"

"Marjorie Clark? Doesn't mean a thing."

"She arrived yesterday on one of those 48-hour airline specials and has to be back at Glasgow airport by seven o'clock tomorrow," Ruth said, drawing his usual pint. "Said she used to live at the old Benton farm when the inn was run by your dad. She had to pass the inn when she came home from school."

"Must've been years ago. Dad's been gone a long time and Benton's is a ruin."

"You would frighten her by yelling at her and chasing her up the lane towards the farm, she said. Bit of a terror, eh, when you were a lad?"

"I don't know about that," he said, grinning.

"Shall I tell her you're here?"

"Aye, why not?"

A young couple occupying a small table in a corner stood up to leave. He grabbed their chairs, then sat down and began chatting with a couple of acquaintances about the ups and downs of the haulage business, always down at this time of the year. People liked to move house in the spring, not when winter was closing in.

In a few minutes, Ruth was back with an older woman wearing a blue skirt and a white blouse. The stranger was of medium height and on the plump side, and her short black curly hair was streaked with white around the temples. Her face struck no chord in his memory.

"Marjorie Clark," Ruth said as Johnny stood and pulled out a chair. "Guess you two have a lot of catching up to do." She returned to the bar.

Laughter lines fanned from the corners of Marjorie Clark's dark eyes and her fresh complexion contradicted the white in her hair. "It's Marjorie Wilson now," she said, taking his hand in a firm, friendly handshake. Her English accent was overlaid with a faint twang, and he noticed that her voice held laughter at the back of it, as if she laughed a lot. "I'm glad to see you, Johnny McPherson, after all these years. I recognized you right away."

"Sorry, I don't remember you at all. Can I get you a drink?"

"Shandy, please. I was seven when Mum rented the farm labourer's cottage on the Benton farm, and ten when we left in 1969. As a matter of fact, tonight is the thirty-third anniversary of my last night here. September 30th. For some reason, I never forgot the date."

"Nineteen sixty-nine? I'd be thirteen then. Care for some prawns?"

"Just the shandy, thanks," she said; then added, smiling, "It's your height and your hair that gave me the clue."

"Aye, a red-headed beanpole Dad used to call me." As a kid, he'd hated his red hair, but his long legs had come in handy in the days when he'd played soccer. He added, "Ruth says I used to chase you up the lane? Sorry, I just don't remember."

"You terrorized me during my first few weeks here, then I took avoiding action," Marjorie smiled. "I was scared to death of you."

"I wonder why I picked on you? I don't think I terrorized anyone else."

While he waited for Norm to fix the shandy, he studied her reflection in the bar mirror. Although she wasn't conventionally pretty, her face radiated such lively intelligence that it lent an illusion of beauty. She was gazing about her, smiling candidly into the curious faces of his neighbours. Tourists were a rarity, for the village of Kilnevin was too small and off the beaten track to interest the usual visitor to western Scotland.

"It's too bad there's Bingo tonight," he told her when he returned with the drinks. "My wife Ann or my mother-in-law might've remembered you. Ann's maiden name was Crombie."

"Ann Crombie. I remember an Annie who lived next to the school and had shoulder-length black hair." Flashing a grin, she added, "I remember worrying that she'd grow her hair down to her waist, like mine. Pure conceit, I'm afraid."

"That was Ann!" he exclaimed, suddenly pleased, as if he'd discovered that there was a link between them, after all. "And she did grow it to waist-length when she was, I don't know, eighteen or so. She's got spiky blonde hair now."

"We lost my dad when I was seven, so I guess that's why Mum came up from London and rented the cottage, needing to sort her life out."

As well as installing neon lighting, Norm had bastardized an old whitewashed wall by adding plastic beams dented to look like the real thing. Averting his gaze, Johnny said, "There's been a lot of changes since you lived here. The old family farms are dying out and a lot of city folks have bought cottages for use at the weekend. Benton's farm has been a ruin for years."

"I saw that when I visited it this morning. It really hurt, seeing something I loved reduced to rubble."

Surprised, he saw that she meant it.

"Our little cottage was part of the farmhouse," she went on. "On the right-hand corner, if you faced the village."

"The farm labourer's cottage? Yes, I've a vague memory of that."

Several neighbours were glancing their way and he knew that he would have to introduce her soon or risk gossip getting back to Ann.

"I loved it," Marjorie was saying. "I was alone but never lonely. I made friends with the sheep and the hens scratting around the farm, and Charlie the cart horse, and there was a tiny stream where I could paddle and sail paper boats. I could look down on the village, and your house stood out, it being the inn with the Nevin river flowing behind it. I don't know, every time I looked down at the village, I seemed to feel such a ..." She hesitated, then said, "Such a harmony with it, as if I belonged. At least the view from our old cottage is still the same ... and your Scottish accent." She laughed, and he saw she had what he called, "smiley eyes," where a light seems to start way back, brightening until the whole face glows. "The only part of our cottage left standing is the doorway," she continued. "Farmer Benton fixed up a swing there for me, and I would sit in it for hours, just watching the village, and the cloud shadows passing over the fells, and sometimes I'd see a little figure, and it would be you, kicking a ball around the inn's parking lot."

"That's right!" he laughed, remembering. "I was crazy about sports when I was a kid."

"I always thought you looked so unhappy."

"Who, me?" he asked. Nobody had ever said this to him before. "Come to think of it, I suppose I was." Surprised by the revelation, he said, "It was no fun, being the only bairn when your parents had to run a pub seven nights a week." A memory floated up of himself as a youngster, listening to the distant chatter and singing of the grown-ups, while he was shut away in the silence of the back room with only his homework for company. She's right, he thought, I was unhappy.

A middle-aged couple suddenly entered on a blast of wind, the woman noticeable in a big grey hat tipped up at one side. Sadie and Bob Brough, Johnny thought, averting his gaze. Sadie was the local midwife, notorious for keeping her hat on during the birthing process and for delivering gossip more efficiently than she delivered babies.

Marjorie moved her chair out of the draught and sipped her shandy. "I'm not surprised you don't remember me," she smiled. "After I realized you were lying in wait, I'd dodge behind a tree or around a corner, and for three years I tried to make sure you never saw me."

"You succeeded," he said, seeing out of the corner of his eye Sadie's inquisitive stare. Johnny McPherson, he could hear her thinking, chatting up a strange woman while his wife's away.

Marjorie laughed, a throaty chuckle so infectious that faces turned to smile at them. Her laughter unleashed a sudden strange joy within him so that he too found himself laughing. Sadie's stare sharpened, and he cut his laughter short. Sadie could take an innocent reputation and disembowel it in one minute flat.

"Wasn't your bedroom over the front entrance?" Marjorie was asking.

"It was indeed."

"I saw you once, looking out. I thought you were coming to get me, and I was so scared I dropped the library books Mr. Mawson had given me, and broke all records racing home."

"Hey, sorry about that," he grinned.

She smiled, "D'you remember Mr. Mawson? We called him 'Old Maggie.' It's thanks to him that reading's now my favourite hobby."

"Mine too," he said. "You're right, it's thanks to Old Maggie." He nearly added, "Too bad he hadn't inspired Ann as well," but then he thought that's unfair. Although she didn't share his interest in books, compared with some marriages he'd seen, he and Ann had a reasonably good relationship.

"And now you live in Canada?" he said. "Not to get away from me, I hope!"

They laughed again. Her eyes, he saw, were not brown after all, but a warm, clear hazel.

"Unlike me, Mum never liked Kilnevin," Marjorie said. "She claimed you couldn't say hello to a man without hearing the next day that the two of you were having an affair."

"That's one thing that hasn't changed." Raising his voice for Sadie's benefit, he added, "The biggest excitements in Kilnevin are bingo and scandal-mongering."

"After '69, Mum moved back to London. That's where I met my husband, Jack. He's red-headed like you, only not so red, more of a ginger. Jack taught science at the high school where I taught

English. We've got a son and a daughter now, both of them in Australia, and she's just got herself engaged to an Australian so I guess she'll be staying permanently. You've finished your drink, may I buy you another?"

"No, you're my guest. Ann and I have two sons, one divorced already, sad to say. We celebrated our silver wedding anniversary some time ago. Pretty miraculous, I suppose, these days."

"Oh well," she said vaguely, "you jog along, don't you? You jog along."

Jog along, he thought. Yes, that summed up his relationship with Ann. When he'd been a teenager, young people had had to look for a partner among their few peers in the village. It was different nowadays. Even teenagers had cars and could find a sweetheart in the wider world of the neighbouring towns.

Marjorie had a very easy smile. Her teeth were small, a little crooked but very white. She had finished her drink. "Can I get you another?" he asked.

"Not just yet, thanks. You know, this is my first trip back since Jack and I emigrated. D'you know what happened to Elaine Hutchinson ..."

The accuracy of her memory was astonishing. They went through a list of familiar names and gradually, he forgot about drinks or that he should introduce her to his neighbours. A few old-timers had remained in the village, he told her, but most of them had scattered like leaves before the wind. Some he had actually forgotten, and it was she who had to remind him. The enjoyment he felt talking to her was astonishing.

"You were born here, you've sent down roots," she was saying. "I'd love that. I can't settle. Jack and I, we roll around like a couple of tumbleweeds. Toronto to start with, then Montreal and then a few more cities. Even Australia for a few months. In fact, in a week or so we'll be returning. Jack's been offered a partnership in a business, and now that our daughter's getting married it'll be an extra incentive to stay. That's why I dashed over here now, because if we start a new life in Australia I don't think I'll ever be able to afford this trip again."

"Fancy travelling all the way from Canada just for the weekend!"

"It's the strangest thing, but Kilnevin keeps pulling me back."

"I think Ann would prefer your life. She thinks Kilnevin is a dead end. And I must admit I get a bit restless myself sometimes." Out of the blue, he added, "Sometimes I feel as if I'm searching for something, but what it is, I haven't a clue. Daft, eh?"

Hearing himself give voice to the confused sadness that sometimes surfaced from deep within him, he suffered a ridiculous desire to bawl like a baby. Embarrassed, he turned his head away and saw that his neighbours, particularly Sadie, were openly staring at him. Annoyed, he stood up. Without asking Marjorie if she'd like another drink he fetched her a shandy and a beer for himself.

It was time to introduce Marjorie to the neighbours. If he didn't, the gossips would spread the word that Johnny McPherson didn't want anyone meeting his unknown companion. In this, he was helped by Marjorie herself. She had a way of putting people at ease, a manner that seemed to say, Hello, I'm glad to meet you, I'm interested in you, tell me about yourself. Watching her laughing with a group at a neighbouring table, he realized that she was an extraordinarily vibrant and charming woman.

Gradually, people returned to their own small circles. He found he was glad when they moved away. Now he could concentrate on this stranger whom he seemed both to know and yet not know.

"This is the first time you've visited Kilnevin since you left?

"Oh no, I cycled through on my seventeenth birthday. July '76. But I only stayed a couple of hours. As a matter of fact, I saw you and you spoke to me."

"I did? What, all those years ago?

"It was in the morning. I'd parked my bicycle against the inn ... now isn't that funny, fancy parking there when I was hoping I wouldn't see you! Suddenly, there you were, walking up the road. I remember thinking, 'Oh no, Johnny McPherson!' so I took out my map and kept my head down." She ducked her head in imitation, and he caught the faint flowery perfume of her hair before she raised her head again and continued, "I hoped you wouldn't recognize me. As you went past you asked, 'Are you lost?' and I mumbled, 'No, I'm not lost, thank you,' and you said, 'I'm not lost either,' which silenced me altogether, I can tell you! To my relief, you disappeared into the inn. I cycled up to the Benton farm, then cycled home."

"Sounds like I was a right know-it-all," he grinned. He'd have been twenty then, and going out with Ann.

"You were dressed all in black," Marjorie continued. "Even a black tie. I remember thinking you looked as if you'd just come from a funeral."

"What?" he burst out. "That would've been Mr. Crombie's funeral! July 10th! I'll never forget the date, because Ann and I got engaged that evening and Dad was furious. He said we were far too young and that it was only the funeral that made us think

68

we wanted to get married. You were there that morning? I actually spoke to you?" He stared at her, amazed.

"Funny, isn't it? Jack and I also drove through the village just before we left for Toronto in 1990. I just had to have one last look. We didn't stop though. Jack's not one for sentiment and the kids were whining. I saw a black Bentley in front of the inn, and I thought the driver had red hair, but Jack wouldn't stop to let me make sure."

"I had that old Bentley for years!" he cried. "Good God! You'd made a special trip from London? I've only been there once, when Glasgow was playing Liverpool for the Charity Soccer Cup, in '88."

"Jack and I were there too. We saw the Glasgow supporters waving their scarves, so I insisted we join them."

"Then you could've been standing only a few feet away from me."

"And if only I'd turned my head, I would've seen you!"

They laughed together.

"Ever been to Canada?" she asked.

"Unfortunately, no. Ann hates travelling. We usually holiday locally. We've only been abroad once, to Nice, because for some reason or other I'd set my heart on visiting the French Riviera. We flew from Glasgow. That was in '95, the last two weeks in August. Excelsior Hotel, Rue Anglaise, very smart."

"Good Heavens, so did we! We were living in Canada by then and returned via Glasgow. How funny if you'd had the room next to ours, but while we were eating in the dining room, you were eating on the patio."

"Or while we were coming in via the front entrance," he laughed, "you were exiting via the back."

"Or, when we flew back to Glasgow, you were sitting in the front of the plane, and Jack and I were in the rear."

"I nearly missed you tonight too," he grinned. "I only dropped in on impulse."

Their laughter had attracted Sadie's attention. Rising, she squeezed past on the obvious pretext of talking to friends at a neighbouring table while her sideways stare ate Marjorie up. Her grey upswept hat looked like a dorsal fin. Glancing at Marjorie, Johnny thought, I'm glad I didn't miss you this time, I really like you. However, he wouldn't say that out loud, not with Sadie circling like a hungry shark. Avoiding the midwife's avid gaze, he rose to order another shandy for Marjorie and another beer for himself.

"Not for me thanks, Johnny," she smiled. "Otherwise I'll be up and down all night."

Her words brought him up short. Two was the legal limit, but just lately he'd been pushing it, sometimes buying a bottle of the hard stuff to drink at home.

"I suppose I'd better not, either," he said, sitting down.

"I'll get some prawns," she said, and was up and at the bar before he could stop her.

"Did you have Mr. Stevenson as your teacher?" she asked when she returned and placed the plate of prawns between them. She cupped her chin in her hands, smiling at him, the white streaks in her hair glistening under the lights.

"Thanks for the prawns. Didn't everybody have him?" he asked, offering her a paper napkin. "He was the headmaster."

"D' you remember how keen he was on folk music?" she asked, selecting a prawn. "We had to learn a new song every week and sing it in the vernacular. He used to call them 'Oor —"

"Oor heritage," he trumpeted, imitating Mr. Stevenson's fruity tone.

Smiling, she leaned towards him, and sang in a low, clear voice, "Ca' the Yowes, tae the knowes —"

"Ca' them whar the heather grows," he joined in, "ca' them where the burnie rows, my bonnie dearie." Call the ewes to the hillocks, call them where the heather grows, call them where the small burn flows, my beloved. He couldn't recall the second verse and was barely able to recall the last verse, but she remembered it.

"Fair and lovely as thou art," she sang softly, "thou hast stolen my very heart. I may die but I canna part, my bonnie dearie."

Their voices must have risen because heads were turning. From the corner of his eye he saw Sadie's hat diving towards them.

"That's the name I gave our cottage," he told Marjorie, lowering his voice. "The Knowes. I must've taken it from that old folk song. Funny, I've never thought of that before."

"Whenever I sing that song, I think of the little River Nevin that flows behind the inn here. That's 'the burnie' to me. And the second verse, where it mentions 'Clouden's woods'? To me, that's the wood on the other side of the village."

"That wood is just behind our cottage."

Once again she cupped her chin in her hands and smiled at him. "My all-time favourite song," she said.

"Mine too. Beautiful words, beautiful melody."

"Do you remember ..."

He followed her as she led him down forgotten childhood paths, recalling this or that incident or an individual in the village. Gradually, he forgot his neighbours in his deep enjoyment of her company. They finished the prawns and continued talking and laughing. At one point, he indicated a collection of photographs on the opposite wall.

"There are some old photos there. Maybe you'll recognize a few faces."

At once she rose to examine them and after a while, he joined her.

"Recognize anybody?"

"Not yet."

"And there are more photos over here," he said, turning.

Every eye was upon them. Sadie was exchanging a knowing grin with Ruth, and this same smirk, he realized, was on every face in the room.

Furious, he returned to his seat, leaving Marjorie to examine the photographs. Typical! They had taken his innocent enjoyment and were trying to make it into something it wasn't. And tomorrow, Sadie and a few of the more vicious old-timers would be telling anybody who'd listen that Johnny McPherson was lavishing drinks on some foreign tart while his wife was out with her mother. And the first person to hear of it would be Ann because the whole village knew that Ann had a dark streak in her, and Sadie got a kick out of stirring things up.

After a while, Marjorie returned to their table. She did not sit down, but remained standing. Everyone was watching her.

"I'd better get some sleep," she said. "It's very late and if I'm not in Glasgow by seven in the morning I'll miss my flight."

Holding out a hand, she smiled, "I've really enjoyed meeting you properly at long last. I do hope it won't be another three decades before we meet again."

It was only 9:00 pm but because of those avid faces, he felt relief along with his disappointment that she was leaving. Rising, he shook her hand. "I've really enjoyed meeting you too," he said, adding firmly, "I too hope it won't be another three decades," even though he knew that Sadie would rip this remark apart and reassemble it into something it wasn't, and that this, too, would be reported to Ann.

The smile Marjorie gave him was strangely uncertain. Then she was gone.

Although he would have preferred to leave, he joined in a game of darts, chatting about this and that, and brushing off his neighbours' sly questions about Marjorie. At last he said, "Ann's probably home by now so I'd better say goodnight," adding deliberately, "I want to tell her about meeting an old childhood friend of hers."

Outside, a pine-scented wind lightly laced with rain blew in his face. From the towering darkness of the fell behind the inn, sheet lightning flared, momentarily revealing the white bones of the ruined Benton farm. Black clouds were shuttering and un-shuttering the moon, so that his truck stood sometimes in moonlight, sometimes in darkness.

As he searched for his keys, Marjorie's voice called quietly above him. "Johnny!" She was leaning out of his old bedroom window, her blouse a glimmer of moonlight, her face a pale oval against the darkness of the unlit room behind her. "Being in your old room reminds me of a silly trick I played on you thirty-three years ago this very night," she said, her voice soft with laughter.

"What trick?" he called.

"I was convinced I'd never see you again, so I guess that's what gave me the courage. It was the night before we left the village forever. A light rain was falling, and there were black clouds racing across a full moon, and a cold wind blowing the world away, just like it is tonight. Mum had taken me to say goodbye to some friends of hers, and we didn't leave their cottage until after midnight. All the village was in darkness, including the inn here. I saw your window in the moonlight."

The hair was rising on the back of his neck. Confused, he asked, "Did you throw a stone through it or something?"

"No!" she laughed softly. "Remember an old American old folk song Mr. Stevenson taught us called, 'Johnny, I Hardly Knew Ye'?"

"Yes," he said. "It's a lament for things lost and gone forever."

"Well, I don't know why, but all of a sudden, I began singing the song out loud, only I changed it to 'Johnny, I Hardly Knew You.' Mum had to drag me away. She was so mad at me! I didn't wake you, then?"

"No," he said, "you didn't wake me."

"Maybe it was just as well. Goodbye, Johnny. God bless."

"God bless you too."

She drew back. The sash rattled, and the window became an oblong of silvered darkness.

The following morning dawned windy but fine. He drove to his appointment in Glasgow, and around noon, dropped into a pub where he had arranged to meet a friend from Kilnevin. Alec had already heard about Johnny's spending the evening flirting with a strange woman.

Johnny snorted, "By God, this has got Sadie Brough stamped all over it! I was just talking to Marjorie about old times, that's all. I never expect to see her again."

"It wasn't Sadie, it was Ruth. She was telling me she'd forgotten to ask Marjorie to write her address in the register, so now she can't send her a Christmas card, like she does to her customers every year. What part of Canada is that Marjorie from?"

"I don't know. She never said and I didn't ask. In any case, she's moving to Australia."

"Ruth's had it, then. Seems like you and that Marjorie caused a bit of gossip, eh?"

Marjorie's strangely uncertain smile when she'd told him that it was late and she had to leave rose before him. So she, too, had seen the smirks, had read those faces, greedy for any bit of scandal that would spice up the day-to-day boredom. She had seen his discomfort and had gracefully withdrawn in order to save him further embarrassment.

It was mid-afternoon when he drove home over the fells. His restlessness had returned. Often he sighed, as if he couldn't get enough air, and he had to force himself to concentrate on the traffic. A couple of miles outside Kilnevin, he passed the side road that wound past the old Benton farm, and on impulse, turned the truck around. When had he last driven this way? He couldn't remember. Pulling up beside the ruined farmhouse, he switched off the engine and sat staring at the weedy mounds of fieldstone and slate. The farm labourer's attached cottage had occupied the far corner; now, only a grass-filled hollow indicated the location of the living room, and, as Marjorie had mentioned, a stone rectangle was all that remained of the front doorway.

He climbed out into the scent of heather and the quiet music of rippling water. Picking his way between scattered fieldstones, he located a narrow golden-brown burn rustling down the fell, with here and there a shallow pool large enough for a child to paddle in. For long minutes he stared at it, imagining Marjorie entertaining herself with a paper boat; then he turned to look down on the village. Smoke was streaming from the huddle of chimneys; the inn itself was clearly visible with the River Nevin glistening behind it. To the inn's left was the parking lot where he had practised his soccer skills so many years ago. On the far side of the village stood the whitewashed oblong of The Knowes, the cottage that he and Ann had bought together. Further back were the moving white dots that were sheep racing through the cloud shadows, and further back still, the dark, deep wood that Marjorie had christened Clouden's Woods.

The words of the second verse that he thought he had forgotten opened within him: "Hark the mavis' note and clang, soondin' Clouden's woods amang, there a-fauldin' let us gang, my bonnie dearie" Listen to the thrush singing in Clouden's Woods. Let us go there and make love, my beloved.

Suddenly, his world wavered and he seemed to lose his grip on the day. Everything was moving away from him: the streaming smoke, the racing sheep, the burn flashing a silver semaphore as it hurried towards the Atlantic, the clouds and their shadows fleeing westwards over the fells and out of sight.

Turning, he stared at the ruin of the farm labourer's cottage before clambering towards it over the weedy mounds. Protruding from one mound was a sliver of wood, flakes of faded brown paint still clinging to its surface: all that remained of a window frame, perhaps, or a door. Not understanding why, he picked it up and slipped it into his breast pocket, then stood within the stone rectangle that had been the cottage doorway. His heart swelled and began pounding.

And there, in the splintered door lintel: two rusty iron hooks, swollen into layers by decades of sun, rain and snow. When he touched a hook it crumbled immediately on his fingers, leaving a brownish-crimson smear, like blood.

He returned to the truck, but did not switch on the ignition. For long minutes he sat with his stained fingers on the steering wheel, sometimes staring at the ruined farmhouse, sometimes at the inn below.

Night, he was thinking, a light rain falling, black clouds racing across the moon, a cold wind blowing the world away. Night, a light rain falling, black clouds racing across the moon, a cold wind blowing the world away. Night, a light rain falling, black clouds racing across the moon, a cold wind blowing the world away.

He switched on the ignition; switched off.

Night. A light rain falling. Black clouds racing across the moon. A cold wind rattling his bedroom door, waking him; rain gusting through the open window and spattering over the planked floor. And suddenly, borne to him on the wind, the clear, sweet voice of a girl. Then the scramble out of bed and his hiding behind the curtain so that he wouldn't be seen. And standing on the other side of the road, a young girl made of moonlight, her waist-length black hair flying about her, her arms lifted to him and singing "Johnny I Hardly Knew You"; singing to him, the thirteen-year-old Johnny, and the wind bringing her voice to him like a gift, and the pine-scented rain sweet on his lips and a wild joy

77

taking all of him, so that his whole body began to tremble with he knew not what. He had not recognized the girl.

But, he knew now, he had been searching for her ever since.

A GIFT FOR MICHAEL MOONEY

Because Hansen hated flying, he and Michael were taking the evening ferry from Tsawwassen to Swartz Bay in Vancouver Island, where they would spend the night. A sales chart, stamped "Hansen Heavy Equipment" lay on the seat between them, its graph angling upwards. His long-lipped mouth working busily, Hansen was extolling the new sales policy, which entailed firing the salesman with the fewest sales at the end of every month. "Gets them off their fuckin' butts," Hansen had said, pinning up the chart that tracked each man's progress. Michael's mouth felt full of dust. Yes, sales had zoomed. It had also turned the sales staff against one another. Nowadays, the fear in the office was palpable as those at the bottom fought not to be the man given the shove. Because he was the sales manager, it fell to Michael to do the shoving.

Oblivious to passersby, Hansen had closed his eyes and thrust his stubby legs into the aisle. Michael had the window seat. Coastal mountains raised a jagged black spine against the moon-lit night, and the Georgia Strait was a yawping blackness except where it was laced by whitecaps. Glistening silver-white in the moonlight, the whitecaps looked like an altar cloth laid over the darkness of the world.

"The new policy goes into the contract, okay?" Hansen grunted without opening his eyes. "Then we can promote the Pave-O-Matic One-Four-Four."

"We'll go go go!" Michael said, repeating one of his boss's slogans.

Passengers' voices mingled with the rumble of the ship's engines. Michael's feet were suffering pins and needles, and even his fingers held a steady tremor, as if his body were merely an extrusion of the ferry. When Hansen reached for yet another sales report, Michael waited; however, his boss remained silent. Lifting his tape recorder, Michael turned a shoulder to Hansen in order not to disturb him and leaning towards the window murmured, "Donna, send this one to Jackson's Road Machinery in —"

Something was glowing in the darkness. He glanced towards it, his lips already forming the word "Toronto." What he saw, gleaming mother-of-pearl amidst the moonlit whitecaps, were the head and shoulders of an enormous horse.

His lips froze about the arriving syllables. The communal language of passenger and ferry passed away.

Pearly forelegs ending in great silver hooves burst through a wave and reached for a whitecap. The horse began pulling itself out of the sea. Michael saw a long glistening back and powerful haunches ending in a massive, shimmering tail and long, feathery tail fins. Wheeling in the same direction as the ferry, the horse began diving and reappearing, keeping pace. Rainbows flew from the streaming mane; from the tail, foam flew like blown snow. The great neck turned and the head moved from side to side, as if the horse were searching the ferry's windows.

A trembling struck up in Michael's flesh. Without taking his eyes from the horse, he touched Hansen on the arm.

"Huh?"

"Look," Michael whispered.

Hansen's face puckered up. He was twinned into the same type of expensive business suit as Michael: navy blue three-piece, white silk shirt and red tie, although Hansen's tie was of a bloodier hue. Removing his glasses, he leaned towards the window so that Michael was treated to a potpourri of talcum and aftershave. The ferry was beginning to pitch in a heavy swell.

"What?" Hansen asked.

The horse was leaving the ferry behind, its forelegs and long powerful tail a shimmering ballet against the darkness, its feathery tail fins rising and falling like the veils of a bride.

"What ... what do you see?"

"What d'you mean?" Hansen frowned, jamming on his glasses. "Hey, this fucking boat is bouncing!"

The horse was dancing on a swell, looking back as if waiting for the man-made thing to catch up.

"Jeez, how many lifeboats does this thing have?" Hansen asked nervously, elevating his pale eyebrows at Michael.

"Got to go to the washroom," Michael mumbled.

Inside the cubicle, he threw up and then leaned his forehead against the cold comfort of the Formica partition. He hadn't touched any booze, he didn't do drugs and he'd had his yearly physical only a month ago. "What the hell?" he whispered.

Some minutes later, he returned to his seat. Hansen, scowling over sales sheets, moved to let him pass but did not speak. Michael pressed his face to the window. Patches of fog had appeared, and in the darkness between them the lights of a coastal town glimmered their faint and fragile gold. And there, a celebration of pearl and silver in the moonlight, was the horse, weaving and diving between the fog patches, light streaming from its body and tail.

"I'm not satisfied with Benson's performance," Hansen was grumbling. "He's had Mansini Distributing for a month and he's still not got an order. Get rid of him."

Dragging his gaze from the horse, Michael got out, "Ed Benson's ... been pretty sick ..."

"We can't play fucking nursie any longer. Chuck him and give Mansini's to George Jones."

"But Ed's ... got kids ..."

"Shoulda pulled his socks up, then, shouldn't he?" grunted Hansen. He grabbed at a pen that had begun to clatter against the side of his briefcase.

Michael turned haggard eyes towards the window. His stomach loosened. The horse had drawn much nearer, enabling him to see it more clearly. It was a stallion and its length from ears to tail fins must have measured forty feet. Hooves reflected silver arrows back to the moon; the enormous tail fins shone sapphire when they lifted clear of the water and opaline when they swept beneath. Sweating coldly, he saw the lustrous head turn and two blue-green jewelled eyes search the ferry. There could be no doubt that the horse was looking for something or someone. It had moved slightly ahead but was gazing leisurely and deliberately down the length of the windows. Swallowing, Michael waited. Then the horse found him. Up went the great silver hooves as the horse reared, and it seemed almost to applaud as Michael's window drew level. Michael's mouth opened and a sound wheezed out. Throwing back its head as if in reply, the horse opened its shining mouth, and although he heard nothing, Michael knew that it had whinnied. Then the horse plunged its head into an oncoming whitecap, its back arched and the great shining tail, terrifying in its enormity and beauty, rose vertically into the air and sank beneath the waves.

Michael had no clear memory of how he coped with the remainder of the crossing.

On his return to Vancouver he insisted he have another physical, citing extreme exhaustion. Pressing and prodding, Doctor Hunter mused about ulcers and the stress of today's downsizing on the business executive, and then recommended a change in diet; possibly, he suggested, even a change of career.

"I'm forty-one, I can't switch careers now. Besides, my salary is excellent. Frank, I was just wondering ..."

Offhandedly, he asked about the effects on the mind of watching television shows such as *The Twilight Zone*. The doctor only half-listened to Michael, but when pressed, remembered a couple of television studies.

Their local library had only one book on the subject. Michael read it, then returned it none the wiser and left with several books on psychology and the male climacteric or andropause. These he speed-read in his office during the lunch break, so that he wouldn't have to parry questions from his wife, Joan. Lately, her tongue had developed a razor's edge.

The articles on the andropause helped not at all, while the accounts of other people's hallucinatory experiences carried him into a world of horror ... the monsters that could stalk the psyche! Giant rats, pythons ... what had he to do with aberrations such as these? Besides, his horse had not been monstrous, but beautiful. Yet each description of the monsters experienced by others seemed to touch something within him, as if he were a distant relative to the mentally deranged. In the torment of the small hours they advanced upon him, misshapen souls beckoning from their warped world, their sly voices inviting him to rejoin the family.

He found himself telling Joan, "I'm thinking of leaving Hansen's."

"Are you utterly mad? You fought to get that job!"

Why had he said a crazy thing like that? And to Joan, who was a worrier!

"I ... er ..."

Defying both sets of parents, they had married at nineteen while he was still studying for his teacher's certificate. Why had he been so set on marrying her? Because she was the double of the beautiful film star Elizabeth Taylor. It had seemed a splendid reason at the time.

"Don't be an idiot, Michael," she shrilled, indicating their cedar and glass living room. "You left teaching because you yourself said the big money was in sales!"

"The doc suspects I'm getting an ulcer ..."

"Then take a holiday! Listen, you're due to take over Walter's position when he retires. Don't give up, Michael, not when we're starting to afford all the nice things we've always wanted!"

"I think we've got enough already —"

"But it's not paid for, is it?"

Her temper was rising, her lips tightening into the all-too-familiar thin line; her violet eyes darkening, yet with a flame at the back of them "What's got into you, Michael? Are you forgetting our sons? What about university fees? And what about me? I could've taken a sound degree in science, but I stayed home to look after you all, didn't I? That was because you asked me to."

Did this slowly burgeoning enmity happen in most marriages? It was true; he had asked her to stay home. That was the political correctness of two decades ago: Wifey stays home and makes everybody comfortable while hubby brings home the bacon.

The following morning he fired Ed Benson; in the evening, he drank himself stupid. He was too befuddled to know if it really was Ed trembling in the doorway, or whether the white-faced salesman was merely a projection from the nightmares that were beginning to trouble him.

"You tell that bastard," the hazy figure said, "that one of these days, he's toast. Okay? You tell that bastard that."

But Michael convinced himself he'd only suffered yet another nightmare.

A week later, when he and Hansen were on the trial ferry run from Tsawwassen to Seattle, the horse danced towards them out of the moon.

Michael turned a bloodless face to Hansen. "Sorry," he mumbled, "what did you say?"

A frown was working Hansen's face. His glasses flashed. "For Chrissake pay attention, Mooney," he grunted. "Your face has been stuck in that fucking window ever since we got on this boat. I said we're gonna have to cut the commission from three per-cent to two."

"But ... the contracts ..."

"We'll renegotiate. Or else."

In the seat in front of Hansen a woman read a novel, her face drawn in concentration. Beside her, a little boy was pushing a red truck around the window, whispering to himself. Michael could see one enormous tail fin flashing beyond the truck's wheels. The ferry began to pitch.

On came the public address system. "Good evening, ladies and gentlemen. Captain Bourque here," a carefully casual voice intoned. "We seem to have encountered ... oh, just a lee—ttle bit of a rough sea. Please remain seated until further notice. Those on the port side will see the lights of Tsawwassen if they look now."

The address system clicked off. With the languid movement of a placid wave flowing up a beach, passengers on the left-hand side turned to look out of the windows. At the same time, the lights flickered and went out. And there, clearly visible through the port-side windows, was the horse, leaping and diving in the moonlight. Surely to God, Michael thought, his hands trembling against his seat, surely someone ...

"San Francisco," Hansen's voice pronounced in the darkness. "We've got to smarten up the distributor there, Mooney."

Someone has to see it, Michael thought, I can't be the only one.

86

The lights came on again and passengers turned back to papers and magazines. Some settled their heads against their seats, trying to snatch some sleep. In a minute, however, the ferry began shuddering violently.

"Hey, what the fuck —" began Hansen. But Michael wasn't listening. Instinctively, he had pressed his face to the window. And his instincts were right: the horse had dived under the ferry and re-emerged on the starboard side. It was plunging towards him, its great tail lashing the sea into phosphorescent falling stars. Then it paused, the pearly head lifted, and it seemed to Michael that even though the lounge was crowded, the horse had singled him out, as if the sea creature's gaze and his were drawn irrevocably towards each other like lovers. Dimly, he heard Hansen's voice snorting and blowing like something feeding from a trough, but all his attention was on the horse. Up went the silver hooves, body and tail rose out of the water amidst streams of phosphorescence and the horse pirouetted, turning so that it hung like a great gleaming jewel against the night before crashing into the sea.

"Mooney, will you get your head out of that fucking window! I asked what promotions you're planning for the Spreader Two-Twenty?"

"The truth is, the truth ... sick ... can't talk ..."

"Really? Sorry to hear that," Hansen said, his gaze sweeping over Michael, as if there were clues to be picked up from Michael's undistinguished nose, his receding hairline, his thinning sandy hair. "Bit sudden, isn't it? Hey, you're shivering! Jeez!" Hansen's pupils suddenly expanded in affront. "Mooney, you're not going to pull a heart attack on me, are you?"

As if mesmerized, Michael was drawn back to the window.

"Just ... just let me sit quietly," he whispered as the horse reappeared and began waltzing in the moonlight. "Just let me rest."

The shining head sank, the great tail flipped skywards and the horse dived. Seconds later, the ferry began to pitch again, causing passengers to exclaim and grasp at their seats and a child to tumble onto his back. Michael closed his eyes and waited, knowing the horse was making for the port side. After a minute or two, he fearfully turned his head to the left. He was right: the horse had reappeared about one hundred yards away. The jewelled eyes flashed towards him and the horse dived once more before reappearing only seconds later about twenty yards away from where it had gone down. It was, he realised, playing a game. A fog bank appeared, pale cloudy ferns knotted to the sea, and the horse leaped between them as some passengers worried aloud about the sudden change in the weather conditions.

"Helluva trip," Hansen said uneasily. "Better not be the Big One."

The Big One was the earthquake predicted to hit the west coast, which was part of the "Pacific rim of fire." If the earthquake occurred in the Strait, it would cause a tsunami.

"Heard a queer thing recently," Michael mumbled. "Some salesman — not one of ours — is telling people that twice — he saw — a huge seahorse playing around the ferry —"

"Christ! Sure glad he doesn't work for me!"

"This man — is supposed to be — the steady type —"

"Booze," Hansen said confidently.

"I believe he — doesn't drink much —"

"Fella obviously needs a break in the worst way."

"Yet he's always been ambitious," Michael said, and then his voice failed.

"Shit!" said Hansen. "You're gonna have to get rid of Sam Yee as well." He brought up a spreadsheet on the laptop screen. "That seahorse," he threw out, "could be a gift from the gods."

"What do you mean?"

"You know, that Greek stuff. My gran had a brass clock decorated with that Neptune fella standing in a chariot and holding the reins of three seahorses. Maybe Neptune just decided to send that sales fella one of his horses."

"But why?"

"For Chrissake, Mooney! Can't you recognize a joke?"

"But why a gift to him? Why him?"

"Maybe Neptune thinks the fella needs to escape," giggled Hansen. "Now for Chrissake let's get on with next year's projections. Better get that fella to a psychiatrist," he said over the top of his glasses. "He's a nut case."

"That's what I'm afraid of," Michael said, and smiled wanly into Hansen's big, pink, healthy face.

At home, Joan took him to task for having mentioned he might leave Hansen's. He reassured her he hadn't meant it, but her furious, frightened probing continued. When, after supper, she threw herself into an armchair, tightly folded her arms and sat glaring at a comedy show on TV, Michael escaped into his study.

For a little while he stood unmoving, then drew in a deep breath, walked to his computer, clicked on to the Internet and typed "Mythology" into the search engine.

The volume of material was overwhelming. Mythological tales, one writer suggested, were about search and discovery, including the quest for a truer self. Often they involved a journey, which could be circular, leaving from and returning to the same place. Science and myth, he read next, represent the left and right hemispheres of our brains and are equally important; they are not, contrary to modern thinking, diametrically opposed. Another click brought up "Science is to myth what we are to our ancestors, a modern rendition of a continuing story," while a search for information on Neptune brought up only that Neptune was the Roman name of the Greek sea god Poseidon, sometimes portrayed as half-man, half-fish, and that he governed the sea. The gods, the writer continued, were believed to interact on occasion with people, a contact that might end in death for the human involved, or alternatively, he/she might be carried to a beautiful, blessed land known as "The Fortunate Isles," where they would enjoy blissful eternal life. All these writings seemed to come to the same incredible conclusion: that an intangible psychic world existed alongside the tangible physical world and that it was every bit as real.

The door flanged open.

"Do you realize how lucky you are to draw such a high salary?"

"Yes, I agree one hundred percent, Joan, it is an excellent salary —"

"Yet you dare talk about leaving!"

"Look, please, don't worry about it. It was a stupid thing to say, please forget it."

"Forget it? How can I? Have you forgotten Hansen's excellent pension scheme?

"Yes, it is excellent."

"And then there's the insurance benefits. If anything happens to you, the boys and I will be well taken care of, and that's vitally important, Michael, because I can't have a career now, can I? All I've got for twenty years of looking after you is homemaker skills, and Big Business doesn't value those, does it, Michael?"

"Look, I wish I'd never mentioned it —"

"But you did mention it," Joan cried, with a bitterness that stunned him. Her eyes were bright with tears. "Women don't realize how they harm themselves by staying home. It's not fair!"

No, it wasn't fair, he could see that. "You're only forty-one, Joan, you're intelligent, you could train for something."

The sudden violence in her face shocked him into silence. After a while, she said slowly, "Oh, thank you very much. You asked me to drop getting my degree, and now you're saying I can train to be something else. A shop clerk? McDonalds, maybe? Thank you, Michael. Thank you very much indeed."

"I — I'm truly sorry, Joan."

She stalked into the living room. Heart sinking at the unpleasant evening ahead, he followed her.

Fearing her reaction, he had not told her about the horse. Nor had he said anything to his two sons, aged sixteen and eighteen, because they took after their mother. Instead, after some hesitation, he visited a psychiatrist and tried to remember all the non-events of what, when he looked back on it, seemed to be his non-life. Had Michael wanted riding lessons as a child and been denied them? Dr. Lynn Georges enquired. No? How about his last name, Mooney? Was he a Kabbalist by any chance, subscribing to the ancient theory that one's fate is linked inextricably to one's name; to illustrate, the moon controlled the tides and a Kabbalist might insist that anyone with Michael's surname had an inborn connection to the sea or to water. No? Had he, she asked suddenly, as if this line of thought led to another, ever been punished for bedwetting?

"None of those things. But in the last few days I've had severe stomach pains. Do you think my stomach problem is triggering off the hallucinations?"

Dr. Georges asked about the colour of his stool — black, perhaps, indicating internal bleeding?

"I've had a physical and everything seems fine, but just lately I've been in real pain."

"Inform your family doctor immediately, okay? In the meantime, think about anything that could link you to horses or to water."

August arrived. Gratefully, he realized that for a whole month he wouldn't have to endure a ferry trip. Meanwhile, the pains in his stomach continued, but an X-ray came up blank, making him wonder if the fiery stabbing was caused not only by his wretchedness at having to sack a man every month, but also because of his worsening relationship with Joan. She seemed intent on dredging up every disagreement they'd ever had, and each quarrel seemed to open the door to another, like an endless passageway of mean little rooms.

During the first week of September, the trip from Tsawwassen to Seattle had to be cancelled because his stomach pains were so severe. Then a trip to Victoria on Vancouver Island came and went without incident, as did another trip in October, crossings that were made during the day. Michael proposed to Hansen that they travel during the day in future.

"No, it's best we keep the day free for meetings. Listen, Charlton Brothers have a new garbage compactor."

"Yes. It's better than our Compactor Four-Thirty."

"Well, we got to get rid of the Four-Thirties whether they do a good job or not. So when we meet with the president of Lancet, we'll offer him a week in Vegas with some T and A thrown in. How's that stomach of yours?"

"They're going to take a biopsy from my bowel. Sometimes I can't move."

"Hey," grinned Hansen, brightening, "tell them to check for ground glass, eh? Us married guys never know if the little woman's decided to polish us off."

"You've got to be kidding!" Michael exclaimed.

Hansen paused to take in Michael's expression, then giggled, "Jeez! Know something, Mooney? You wouldn't recognize a joke if you fell over it."

Three days later, he and Hansen had to visit Victoria, and Michael manoeuvred the schedule so that they would be forced to travel during the noon hour. Hansen seemed oddly restless.

"Queer weather," Hansen said. "Look at the fucking sun. Red. Don't like it."

Michael, too, was unable to concentrate. He and Joan were sleeping apart now. That morning, after a night's severe pain, he had turned to tell her that he was leaving for the office, and for a terrifying second, found himself looking not into the violet eyes of the film star Elizabeth Taylor but into the pitiless eyes of the beautiful and wicked queen from Snow White. Then the face had changed back to Joan's familiar features. He didn't know what had happened or what it meant. He knew only that the moment surfaced again and again as if his subconscious were forcing it on his attention.

"By the way," Hansen tossed out, "We'll be reforming the company pension and insurance schemes. Too rich. Not fair to the shareholders."

Michael noticed how Hansen's solid paunch rounded over his knees.

"My son Brad," Hansen continued, "has graduated top of his economics class. He's looking for a position, possibly in sales." He removed his glasses and his gaze rested on the Hansen logo emblazoned on Michael's briefcase.

A pain began burning Michael's gut; soon, he was shifting in his seat in an attempt to find relief. Blood swelled in his ears, provoking a dull roar in which the passengers' voices were dreamlike ghost-tones of souls lost at sea. Sweat trickled down his forehead and he turned towards the window and mopped discreetly, hoping Hansen wouldn't notice. God, if they couldn't discover the cause of this pain soon! From this angle, the coastal mountains on either side of the Strait were out of sight and the view was of a smooth, endless sunlit sea, giving the impression that the ferry had halted at the edge of the world.

"Brad will go far," Hansen was concluding, his eyes bright. "Chip off the old block. Yes, sales." And when he looked at Michael, the light in his eyes seemed to snap into darkness, as if he had switched Michael off.

Michael suffered another vision. As though a spotlight had been thrown, he saw Hansen's blonde-white hair bristling back from the heavy pink forehead, the big, blunt nostrils jutting beyond the long line of thin upper lip. Behind the glasses, Hansen's eyes were small and yes, pig-like. The vision continued: Hansen, clopping down the gangplank, briefcase clutched in one pink trotter ...

And then he realised that a brilliant light, over and above the reddish sunlight already filling the lounge, was creeping up the blue vinyl of the seat in front of him. At the same time, the ferry began to pitch violently.

The public address system clicked on; the captain's voice said, "Fucking hell," before the tone changed to professional cream and murmured, "Just a little turbulence, ladies and gentlemen. Please remain seated until further notice. Parents are asked to keep their children beside them."

The light was brightening, spreading over the white-painted bulkheads, and it seemed to Michael that the lounge was beginning to smell like a rocky shore at low tide. He did not look out of the window. Instead, he said silently to the shimmering vinyl in front of him, "In the name of Christ, leave me alone."

The pitching intensified.

"Hey, what's that salty smell? Reckon we've hit some sort of storm?" Hansen began nervously, and then the captain's voice cut in, "Attention all crew, all personnel to their —"

The address system went off with a rush. "Shit! Lightning!" gasped Hansen.

The light beyond Michael's window was blinding, as though both the sun and moon were filling the lounge with gold and silver. Two children sitting with their parents began crying, as did an old woman sitting by herself. Foam was streaking across the windows. Slowly, Michael turned his head and what he saw, about ten feet away, as the ferry reared and plunged with its stricken passengers, was an enormous silver hoof. Michael's mind, which had already offered itself up to death, noted almost mechanically that the hoof must be about twelve inches in diameter. Then he saw that there were two hooves: a right and a left, flashing past the window, giant sculptures of silver, dazzling to his eyes ... "Look out the window," he mumbled into Hansen's terrified face. "Look ... look ..."

"It's the Big One!" Hansen screamed, clawing at Michael's sleeve, "God, where's the fucking lifebelts ..."

Children were screaming now, as were many of the passengers. Michael tore away from Hansen's scrabbling hands and suddenly Hansen turned green and threw up into the gangway. The ferry dropped, shot up and slid sideways in a great curtain of foam, and he heard the captain's voice, "Crew ... stations ..."

The hooves were dropping below his vision, and the shining forelegs came into view. Spray was zig-zagging in lacy ribbons down the window; his nostrils stung with the reek of salt. Clinging to the seat as Hansen continued to throw up, Michael saw the horse's coat, each hair lustrous within its own light, as if composed of filaments of pearl. The ferry engines barked as the boat slipped to one side and the stern tipped skywards. Michael's stomach was forced against his ribs as the ferry tore helplessly down a mountainside of water. Passengers were screaming, the seat leaping under his hands, his ears bursting.

A whinnying summons came like a great wind out of space. The ferry dropped like a stone, hurling Michael out of his seat and sending him crashing against other flailing passengers. His forehead smashed against a metal stair and he yelled in agony, lifting both hands to protect his head as blood poured into his eyes. Blinded, he fell across the screaming stranger struggling on the floor beside him before feeling around with bloodstained hands for the stair handrail.

Again came the whinnying summons, louder this time. Somehow, he pulled himself upright and tried to balance his trembling body against the plunging bulkhead as he wiped blood from his eyes. The open doorway at the top of the gangway stairs was shimmering with indescribable effulgence; the reek of salt was choking him.

Once again he heard the long, drawn out, unearthly whinny. Silvery light began spreading down the stairs.

Suddenly, a profound peace opened within Michael, a soul-deep acceptance of what had to be. A man being escorted to the gallows, he felt, might know this same renunciation, might even experience the strange sense of dignity that came to him now. Stepping over the stranger screaming at his feet, he began working his way hand over hand up the stairs and towards the light.

"Mooney ... I'm hurt ... Mooney ..."

A couple of deckchairs cartwheeled past the stairs' open doorway before they splintered against something solid further down. Michael continued climbing.

"Mooney ... my leg ... oh God, Mooney, my leg ..."

The air was a blinding, diaphanous shimmer. The horse's summons was full-throated now, ringing in his ears, powerful, drawn-out chords of unearthly music.

"Yes, I'm coming," Michael whispered. He reached the doorway and stepped onto the splintered chaos of the deck, hair whipping about his bloodied head.

A gigantic whitecap reared up before crashing over the deck

and roaring towards him until he was thigh-deep in swirling, icy foam. Lifting his arms, he held them out towards the glorious creature waiting just beyond the deck rail, and as he struggled forward, he breathed a prayer that his bloodstained hands would have the strength to fasten onto that iridescent mane, and never let go.

THE HOUR OF MISS FRITH

The chill wind snatched up dust, discarded flyers, old bus tickets and Miss Megan Frith of Ladies Hats, and blew them along the sidewalk into Laidler's Department Store. As usual, Miss Frith was the first salesperson to arrive. Other sales staff delayed their arrival at this decaying area of Vancouver until the last minute, and only the young janitor saw the small, grey-haired woman being whirled into the peeling gilt of the staff entrance.

"Good morning, Ben. What unseasonable weather for July!"

She saw his hesitation before he said, "Morning, Miss Frith. Yep, storm's coming."

The hesitation, she knew, was because he was unsure of how to address her. Nowadays, even newcomers addressed their supervisors by their first name. She, however, was from a more formal generation and had worked at Laidler's for so many years that her title, Miss Frith, had stuck.

The ancient brass and iron elevator coughed her up to the staff room on the sixth floor. Opening her locker she hung up her coat, revealing an elegant white blouse and navy wool skirt: a tailored image that took a sharp downturn the instant she slipped into the one-size-fits-all uniform of maroon nylon that was Roberta Laidler's contribution to cost-cutting. Old Mr. Laidler, Ms. Laidler's grandfather, would've had a fit, thought Miss Frith, glancing down at her bag-like shape.

Lifting her purse, she made her way towards the escalator and rode it slowly down into the silence of the store, past flaking cream-painted walls, counters of scuffed oak, chipped green-marble pillars and floors covered in dingy brown linoleum. Each department offered ultra-cheap goods displayed in dreary rows or untidy heaps: furniture held together by staples; pans that burned the minute you turned your back; underwear whose seams ripped at first wearing; T-shirts with dyes that ran at the sight of water; every item manufactured in foreign sweatshops and ordered by Ms. Laidler, who was also the head buyer.

She stepped off at the second floor, where this latest generation of Laidlers had dumped Ladies Hats, Menswear and Ladies Dresses. The dresses offended with shoddy prints and polyesters in the mud- and prune-coloured shades that Ms. Laidler had concluded were the fashion this year, in spite of evidence to the contrary in the newer stores in the city centre. Soon, however, she smiled as if she were greeting a group of old friends. No mad-haired, silver-skinned, flat-chested, sulking twenty-first-century mannequins here. These milk and roses mannequins (her day companions for the last forty years), were ladies in every sense of the word: with delicate, tapering hands and definite (but in no way provocative) curves; their modest gazes looked out from pure oval faces topped by blonde, black or brown painted hair. These ageless ladies looked very much like the ladies from her childhood. Their male counterparts stood to attention across the aisle in Menswear: gentlemen to the core, with noble brows and arrow-straight partings in their smooth plaster hair, heroic types such as those who had stood straight-backed, chin up, on the deck of the *Titanic* while the band played "Abide With Me" and the ship sank to the bottom. That was their hour, she thought. I could die tomorrow and nobody would notice, including me.

The hat department, once so big and busy, had shrunk to a glass counter, presently shrouded by a dustcover, and a large display cabinet with shelves covered by lengths of yellowing white-plastic sheeting. Down went the corners of Miss Frith's mouth. She flicked the dust cover away, revealing cheap Styrofoam heads, white-faced, bald and eyeless beneath ugly hats. Roberta Laidler's dead dreamgirls, Miss Frith thought. Just what was that woman thinking of when she said that only old ladies bought hats? What about Princess Di when she was alive? And would she say that to Ms. Laidler? No, of course she wouldn't say that to Ms. Laidler, Miss Frith told herself, because she didn't have the nerve.

The display cabinet held the final group that summed up Roberta Laidler's view of the older woman. Felt helmets in black, suet-white or puce threatened from the shelves: death and blood-pudding shades that were perfect for women who were to the extreme right of the extreme right. Miss Frith stared at the grim squad lined up in front of her. Not one flirty hat, no froth, no fizz, no fun. No wonder the sales graphs floundered around zero.

A cold draft of air blew through a central heating grate and an envelope lifted from the cash register and floated to her feet.

She hadn't worked for Roberta and Charles Laidler without discovering that whenever anything unpleasant came up (reduced coffee breaks, compulsory unpaid overtime, cancellation of the dental plan) it was the policy of the board to make it known in a letter. Her breath coming a little faster, she ripped the envelope open. *Dear Employee*, began the letter from Charles Laidler, *It is with deep regret that the Board of Directors of Laidler's Department Store Ltd. has decided that owing to declining sales we can no longer operate in the area that has been our home since 1932. The centre of retail activity has moved to West Georgia Street, and it is therefore with great pleasure that we announce our new partnership with the prestigious Hamble Group, which has business interests in that area. Hamble Corporation was established five years ago in Chicago and since that time has successfully expanded across the U.S. and into Canada. Laidler's Department Store Ltd. will be known in future as "The Hamble-Laidler" and will be located in the new Hamble building* ... Charles Laidler stated that the transfer would be completed in eight weeks, that downsizing of staff would be done "as humanely as possible," that the new employment contract "reflecting today's financial realities, would differ in certain respects from their previous contract," and that the Laidler family had no option but to accept an offer for the present building from Asquith and Tong Ltd.

Asquith and Tong! The developers whose purpose in life was to amass property in working-class areas, demolish the small houses and then throw up expensive condominiums! And now

Asquith and Tong was to demolish Laidler's?

Unable to believe it, she reread the letter. Only half a sentence had been considered necessary to assassinate Laidler's, as if the store's seven decades of service to this present generation, their parents, grandparents and great-grandparents, were as nothing. She had seen the new Hamble Corporation building — a hideous circular tower of black glass. The Devil's penis, she had thought when she'd seen it rearing against the sky; a corporate "Fuck you," although nothing would have made her utter such a vulgarity out loud. How could anyone enjoy working in a soul-less place like that? And it was no consolation to know that, along with the small working-class homes vanishing all over the city, such aberrations as the Hamble building would also at some point be flushed down the sinkhole of history.

She sank onto a stool, the letter clutched in her hand. At her fourth rereading her breath quickened, and the print began to blur. What did they mean, "no other option." What options? What effort had the Laidlers made to meet these challenging times with imagination and courage instead of caving in and selling out? Her gaze burned up to the ceiling, where carved plaster rosettes were crumbling like dead flowers, then it went to the shabby brown linoleum and from there to the grim fundamentalist hats. Her fingers trembled over the page.

Other employees arrived and began opening their letters. Soon, raised voices reached her in that place where shock and loss had taken her, and she became aware of the black grave-marker that was Roberta Laidler's business suit. Narrow face alight under blonde hair cut so short and nubbly it resembled puréed sweetcorn, Laidler's head buyer had arrived on the second floor and was holding forth about the glories of being taken over by Hamble. "At last, an opportunity to offer decent merchandise to a good class of customer," Ms. Laidler was exclaiming. "This area should be bulldozed."

Other staff were listening to Ms. Laidler with a pleasure that shocked Miss Frith. Not one person queried the possible demolition of the old store. She couldn't bear it. Had these people no sense of history, no pride?

Uncertainly, she moved towards the head buyer.

That evening, Miss Frith stared blindly out of the window as the bus jiggled her home through shabby streets washed clean by the violent rainstorm that had battered the area that afternoon. All her old griefs had returned to haunt her: Her father's death by drowning, her mother's slow death from cancer, the agonizing loss of her fiancé William to another girl and the even more agonizing death in the womb of the baby she had conceived with him. She thought of her helplessness to change any of these events or indeed anything that had happened to her. And this afternoon her worst fears had been confirmed. Asquith and Tong would demolish the Laidler building as soon as the transfer to the Hamble complex was complete. Her stammered protests "This building is part of Canada's history, it's part of the immigrant experience!" had been met with annoyed surprise by Ms. Laidler and with polite puzzlement by other staff members. Driven by her need, she had dared to ask permission to address Charles Laidler and the board members who were meeting in the boardroom. Politely, they had rejected her halting suggestion that the store was a historic landmark that must be preserved. They assured her that neither the building nor the area was of any architectural interest whatsoever ("City council has not designated Laidler's a heritage building, Miss Frith."), and they pointed out that employees should thank their lucky stars that Laidler's had merged with Hamble and would be moving to Vancouver's most vibrant commercial area. The board had not even referred to the store by name, but as "the package," as if the store had no identity beyond the real estate dollars it represented. She had retreated with apologies for having bothered them.

The bus rattled through the area where she had lived as a child. Closely packed small apartment blocks were gradually taking over the modest houses bought by war veterans with demobilization money. She looked numbly at the FOR SALE signs sprouting like poisonous weeds in the small front yards. Already, only twenty-four hours after one sign had gone up, a crimson SOLD sticker glistened like an open wound.

When she entered the apartment she rented in one of the few remaining Victorian mansions she did not switch on the lamp. A gold aqueous light from the setting sun spread over the bookcase she had inherited from her parents, bringing out the solid oak's rich russet-brown. The oak dining set had also been theirs, items that were common enough in working class homes when she was young, but which were now turning up in antique stores at prices only the well-off could afford.

A movement beyond the window had caught her eye. A building crane stood like a gigantic praying mantis against the sky. Even as she watched, it lifted a ready-cast wall and swung it towards a steel frame, the latest addition to the high rises that had been advancing like a monstrous army from the south.

Turning away, she plugged in the kettle for a cup of tea, not so much because she was thirsty as to drive away the cold that was closing about her.

When the tea was ready she sat in the window seat and viewed the advancing enemy. The sky was now a crimson rash against which Laidler's lighted windows raised their fragile gold, while the small shingled roofs of her own street had darkened to black. She lifted the teacup to her lips.

A great roar, as if from some wounded animal, suddenly tore apart the quiet evening, and only a short distance from Laidler's, the tall, narrow office block known as the Mariner's Building seemed to rise and hover. It floated for several incredible seconds before folding in on itself amidst terrifying cracklings and snappings; then it sank slowly out of sight like a stately creature dealt a mortal blow and buckling majestically to earth. What for eighty years had been a solidity of bricks and mortar was now only a gaping hole beneath a cloud of dust.

Her teacup crashed to the table. She started out of her chair, staring at the pillar of dust rising in tumult against the fiery sky. It was then that she knew that she could not, would not accept the destruction of Laidler's. It would be like surrendering without protest to those powerful forces that had taken hold of her life and shattered it. No, this time she would fight back!

Staring at the boiling pillar of dust, she knew that her hour had come at last.

Two weeks later, Miss Frith was waiting outside Laidler's when the janitor arrived at 6:00 a.m. Sagging from her arms was a bulging carton with a potted fern nodding from the top. The weather was clear and calm; she, however, was all storm inside. There was lots to do before the store opened at 9:00 a.m., lots to accomplish before Charles Laidler and the board members arrived for their weekly luncheon meeting.

"'Morning, Miss Frith," Bob Thompson said, staring. "You look different."

"It's just a little colouring job," she answered, giving her new brunette head a little shake. "This haircut is called a shingle, Bob. I did it myself. It was very popular in the early thirties."

"It was? Jeez! What happened to your eyebrows?"

"Just plucked, that's all. That was the fashion." Taking a deep breath, she asked, "Why don't you call me Megan? Miss Frith is so formal."

"All right, Miss ... Megan."

"Did you do what I asked, that is, what Mr. Laidler asked?"

"Yeah. I done a good job, even if I do say so myself. Hey, what's your perfume, Megan? Sexy!"

Her colour rose. Bob had been so trusting of her forgery of Charles Laidler's signature on the Works Order. "It's called Evening in Paris. It belonged to my mother and I never used it," she mumbled. "See you later."

As she walked carefully into the corridor he called, "Mind you don't trip in them shoes! Where'd you get 'em? The Sally Bash?"

He'd meant it as a joke, she could tell. "Yes," she said into his surprised face, and clacked the strapped black shoes with the long pointy toes into the elevator.

I'm terrified, she thought, as the elevator rattled upwards, but it's gone too far for me to back out now.

In the staff room she stared at her reflection in the mirror, examining the stranger with dark crimped hair who was staring back at her as she inserted a pair of pearl earrings. Pencil-thin eyebrows made her face look rounder, and she was wearing another Salvation Army find, a calf-length, skinny black dress with tight sleeves and a white Peter Pan collar that she'd finished altering the night before.

So much to do. At the thought of what the Laidler family would say such a trembling struck her that her teeth began to chatter. Carrying the carton, she hurried towards the escalator. One of her greatest worries had been resolved yesterday. Roberta Laidler could not be found after 4:30 p.m. but Miss Frith had been terrified that this one time the head buyer might stay until 5:30, as she was supposed to do. However, Ms. Laidler had melted away at the usual early hour, and the big cartons of hats had arrived safely at 5:00 p.m. So had Miss Frith's two oak side chairs (circa 1930) and her potted fern, delivered by her obliging land-lady in her station wagon. Other sales staff, uninterested in anything that went on in the dying store, had not queried any of these peculiar goings-on.

When she arrived at the hat department, Miss Frith halted, her heart pounding. Bob had worked hard. The area had been cleansed of the ugly hats, Styrofoam heads, brown linoleum and yellowing shelf-covering. Before her lay the original gleaming oak parquet floor that she remembered from her early days at the store, and the counter and the display cabinet had been stripped of their tacky coverings, revealing solid polished oak and bevelled glass. Fishing out the photograph of the store that she had photocopied at the Vancouver Museum, she set it where she could use it as a guide. The fern was placed on one side of the counter, her mother's small, embroidered teacloth and silver tea service on the other, and the two chairs at either end. Her fingers were trembling. She could barely remove the tea caddy, the bottles of milk and the big packet of sugar. Two days ago she had made a lucky find in the storeroom: the hat department's original oak hat stands. All they had needed was a good dusting. She soldiered on, arranging her mother's art nouveau cups and saucers in the same hospitable manner as depicted in the photograph. Hurrying into the storeroom, she zig-zagged between the discarded styrofoam heads and placed her electric kettle and caddy of loose tea beside the sink, ready for the customers she was praying today's article in *The Vancouver Sun* would attract to the hat department. Two days earlier she had left a message for Maureen Li of the newspaper's *Living* section informing her of today's event at the store.

At last she stood before the cartons that had arrived yesterday afternoon. It was time for the hats. Not Roberta Laidler's hats. Today's hats.

They blossomed into the air: rapturous yellows, melting pinks, tender blues, naughty scarlets, dazzling whites, ravishing greens: cheeky handfuls or seductive wheeling shapes of silk and net and feathers and veiling and flowers. Taped to one of the cartons was the invoice. She opened the envelope, paling when she saw the sum of money involved, but then her passionate belief in the righteousness of her cause conquered all else. She had been born for this hour: the saving of this beloved building not only for the citizens of Vancouver, but also for every citizen of Canada.

Charles Laidler, a bewildered frown crinkling his forehead, was riding the escalator down to the second floor. Behind him stood his married daughter, Jo Ann Sims, looking equally bewildered. Leading the way was Roberta Laidler, her narrow face alternately swarming with disbelief and outrage.

Charles said, "Are you sure the floor manager has it right? It doesn't sound like Miss Frith at all."

"Bill Campbell wouldn't exaggerate," Roberta said. She turned to stare at her brother. "Forgery!" she exclaimed. "Incredible!" She turned away and immediately turned back. "I made our intentions crystal clear to her," she said. Once again she turned to face the front and once again turned back. "One thousand six hundred and six dollars and forty-seven cents, Bill told me. Sheer, barefaced robbery. What are we going to do with her?"

They arrived at Ladies Dresses and stalked past the sparse number of shoppers and the two silent and apprehensive saleswomen, until at last they rounded a mannequin buried up to her neck in the mud-coloured wool of a winter dress. Ladies Hats was empty except for a woman with peculiar dark hair and no eyebrows.

"Miss Frith," Charles Laidler asked uncertainly, "is that you?"

Then they saw the hats. The hats! Perched on the shelves and counter were scraps of living colour, as if flocks of bright birds were resting among exotic flowers before continuing their journey south. One could almost smell the perfume, hear the rustle of wings.

Charles caught sight of a stack of black and gold boxes with black ribbon handles. He turned to his sister. "H—hatboxes?"

"Three dozen. One hundred and forty dollars."

"Great God Almighty!"

Miss Frith had flushed with fright on seeing the Laidlers. But then her chin came up and she waited silently for them to address her.

Charles stammered, "Miss Frith, I hardly know how — I'm speechless —"

"Well, I'm not," Roberta Laidler said. "I'm assuming you're not drunk, Miss Frith, so what is your explanation?"

Miss Frith's chin lifted. "The store mustn't be closed. We must fight to keep it open."

"We are keeping Laidler's open, Miss Frith, but not down here, and certainly not in this building," Roberta said crisply. "Is that why you've bought these hideous hats? Miss Frith, don't you understand the enormity of what you've done?"

The two saleswomen were lingering nearby, ostensibly tidying the stock, but it was clear that their ears were tuned to the discussion.

"I know it seems incredible, Ms. Laidler, but I was desperate. And I didn't buy the hats, I got them on consignment from Eleanor Capozzi."

"On consignment? Thank God for small mercies," Charles said.

"And just who is Eleanor Capozzi?" asked Roberta.

Miss Frith's eyes opened wide. "She's the fashion designer featured in all the magazines and newspapers!"

"Really?" Roberta stared around the small department, over-flowing with hats and empty of customers. "And have you sold any of Eleanor Capozzi's hats, Miss Frith?"

"Not yet. I was hoping there'd be an article in *The Vancouver Sun* today but apparently there isn't. I'm positive that as soon as the word gets out ... "

"But how will the word get out, Miss Frith?" Charles asked. The eyelid of his left eye began twitching. "There's no way that people around here can afford hats like this. Do you really believe local residents are going to rush over to West Vancouver or Point Grey and tell women, "Listen, you've got to get over to Laidler's and see their hats?"

"I ..."

Charles pressed a hand over his eye in an effort to stop the twitching. "You might be able to sell hats like this in the new store," Charles said. "But not here, Miss Frith. Not here."

"But Mr. Laidler, we can't let this store be pulled down! Our parents shopped here, our grandparents and great-grandparents shopped here. That's what makes it beautiful!"

All three Laidlers stared at her in silence before Roberta asked, "Beautiful? Are you mad, Miss Frith?"

Miss Frith's mouth opened, and the frustration of years poured out. "Yes, I'm very mad, absolutely boiling mad! This is our store, the people's store! What about us? Why do developers always zero in on anything over fifty years old, especially in the areas where poor people live? That doesn't happen in West Vancouver or Point Grey! The people there are safe."

"Because those are beautiful areas to begin with, Miss Frith," Charles said, his eyes bulging because never before had Miss Frith raised her voice. "You can hardly say that about this area. But even if we agreed with you, Miss Frith — and we don't — this store is finished as a viable retail outlet."

Roberta interrupted, "The kindest thing we can do, Charles, is to send Miss Frith home immediately. Miss Frith, I don't think you can be feeling very well. I think it would be a good idea if you went home now and rested, and then in a few days we'll decide on the best course to take."

"Mr. Laidler, you could become famous, putting a well known heritage building before big dollars —"

"That's a totally impractical suggestion, Miss Frith," Charles said.

"Well now," remarked his daughter Jo Ann, coming to life, "Miss Frith may know nothing about finance, but the hats are extremely attractive."

"Only common women would choose hats like that," Roberta Laidlaw snapped.

Down went Jo Ann like a pricked balloon.

"I don't want to be hard on you, Miss Frith," Charles said, "but I agree with my sister. I think you must be ill. You may take the rest of the week off, then we'll get together with the board and discuss if you really want to transfer to the new building on Georgia. All right, Miss Frith? The hats will be returned immediately."

The radiant light of the hour she had regarded as hers darkened, and the cold light of a malignant new day filtered in. The Laidlers and staff members Suzanne Blakeney and Julia Ing stared at her, more with pity than with condemnation. Another kind of darkness, however, shadowed Roberta Laidler's eyes. Hostility and fear. Megan Frith, the ordinary employee, had at least used her imagination in an attempt to save the store, and Roberta Laidler, head buyer and board member, had not. For that, she would not be forgiven.

Miss Frith decided what she had to say. "Thank you, but I don't think I'll be transferring to the new store. In fact, I think it might be a good idea if I put my notice in right now."

"Yes, good idea!" Charles said swiftly as his sister nodded and his daughter frowned. "I don't think you'd be happy in the new store, Miss Frith, I really don't. Suzanne, would you take over here?"

There was nothing more to say. Miss Frith retrieved her purse from beneath the counter and was turning away when, out of the corner of her eye, a hat seemed to step smartly forward and present itself, almost to salute. She paused. It had been love at first sight: the brightest, bravest, cheekiest little scarlet pillbox, with a crimson feather jaunting above one ear — the kind of hat that would be worn by a perky drummer girl. Lifting it, she turned to face a mirror and settled it firmly on her head. The hat perched as rakishly as if she were a soldier back from the war.

She did not hesitate. She looked at the price label, she calculated the tax and in front of the dumbfounded eyes of the Laidlers she dashed off a cheque and deposited it in front of the silent, embarrassed Suzanne. "Your first sale, Suzanne," she said.

She walked past the Laidlers, past the bright flock of hats, past the dumbfounded faces of other sales staff who had heard that something crazy was happening on the second floor, and finally, past the dear, dumb eyes of the plaster mannequins: fellow refugees who soon would be carted off in garbage trucks to their fate.

Bill Campbell, the floor manager, was standing near the elevator. As she passed him he whispered, "Why, Miss Frith? Why?"

"Because," said Miss Frith, "this store is family."

The brass and wrought iron elevator opened to receive her. Stepping inside, she pressed the down button for the last time, then stood to attention, gaze straight ahead, her chin up. The elevator lights flickered and went out; she was submerged in a descending dark, and as she sank her scarlet hat was as a small, brave flag going down under an implacable sea.

MOON CALF

Sunshine brightened and faded and brightened again on flaking white gingerbread trim and fading brown paint. Ann retrieved her briefcase from her Porsche and stood for a minute, examining the shabby little house on the opposite side of the road. She didn't like it. The house was too much like the ramshackle home where she and seven siblings had struggled through childhood.

A headache threatened. She would get the visit over with as quickly as possible, then relax at home.

Dodging potholes, she crossed the road and forced open the gate that barricaded the unkempt front garden. Brambles thrust between the porch steps, threatening her pantyhose as she climbed towards a blistered front door where three doorbells offered a choice of occupants. She pressed the middle button and, as its tinny peal echoed inside the house, turned to examine the view. A chill autumn wind blowing off Burrard Inlet was stripping leaves from the street's few remaining elms, allowing glimpses of cheap stucco apartment blocks interspersed here and there with an old house similar to this one. Straggling hedges trapped discarded flyers, Styrofoam cups and condoms. This area of town was infamous for its prostitute stroll. I don't care how poor people are, she thought as the pages of a newspaper cartwheeled up the street; they could at least clean up the garbage. My sisters and I, we cleaned up the garbage.

She pressed the doorbell again, then attempted to peer through the bay window to her right. Faded crimson velvet drapes shrouded the glass. I'm too tired for this, she thought, I want to go home. For the third, and as far as she was concerned, final time, she pressed the bell.

Immediately, a bolt rattled and the door opened to reveal a grinning, tiny grey-haired woman wearing eyeglasses. A knitted brown dress sagged unevenly above a drooping pink petticoat hem and lace-up brown shoes. From somewhere inside the house rose a man's full-bellied guffaw.

Ann held out her business card. "Mrs. McDougal?" she asked, a little startled by the grin. "I'm Ann Thomas of Investment Securities. Your friend Margaret Chan asked me to deliver some shortbread cookies she's made for you. I'm afraid she's sick and can't visit you today."

"Och, dear!" The old woman removed her glasses and peered into Ann's face "One of her migraines is it?"

Scottish, Ann thought. It's awful when these old biddies let themselves go. She said, "I'm afraid so. She was anxious that I get the cookies to you."

"How kind," the musical voice said. Replacing the glasses, the old woman stepped back and added, "Please come in."

A length of shabby dark hall appeared. "Thanks so much," Ann said gracefully, "but I'm afraid that I ..."

But Mrs. McDougal had vanished behind the door. All that could be seen was a little wrinkled hand, emblazoned with old-fashioned rings, holding the door open. Probably deaf, Ann thought. Stepping forward, she said loudly, "Thank you. I can only stay a minute."

The long, narrow hall was a mirror of her childhood home: same threadbare Turkish carpeting disappearing up a dark flight of stairs, same chipped brown paint, same greyish engravings displayed above a wainscot of embossed brown wallpaper, same smell of damp and cat urine, same sense of defeated small lives draining into history.

The door closed behind her. "You're lucky, my friends are visiting today," Mrs. McDougal piped. "Nola lives upstairs and Dolly has the basement." Rings flashed as she opened another door.

The smells of the hall were also exhaled by the threadbare crimson carpet and armchairs of balding red velvet in the shabby front room. Just like my parents' house, Ann thought as the first threat of a migraine began throbbing at the back of her right eye. A fan of pleated newspaper spread itself in the green-tiled fireplace, oil paintings of Highland cattle and gloomy mountains darkened the fading flowered wallpaper and a coffee table was covered by an embroidered tea cloth that barely hid the pierced concrete blocks doing duty as legs. On the chesterfield behind the coffee table perched two ancient women. One was so brightly garbed it hurt the eye, the other wore the kind of blue butterfly-shaped eyeglasses popular thirty years earlier. Broad grins suggested they had just shared a good joke.

"Girls, meet Ann Thomas," Mrs. McDougal said, pointing up at Ann, a gesture that made Ann feel ten metres high. "Poor Margaret's sick but she's sent some shortbreads, the sweetie."

"That's kind of you to go out of your way like this," said the woman in blue eyeglasses.

Another Scotswoman, Ann thought. "It's no trouble. I pass this street every day on my way home. I live in West Van."

"Och, very posh," Mrs. McDougal said. She nodded at the woman in blue glasses. "That's Nola Currie, and the other lady is Dolly Finlay. Her real name is Mavis, but we call her Dolly."

"Hi," Ann said at the same moment that the two women said, "How do you do?" the o's being pronounced like the French u.

"Sit you down," Mrs. McDougal smiled, indicating an armchair where a loose upholstery spring was pushing its whirlpool shape into the seat. Curved around the whirlpool was a sleeping black cat.

Ann wondered if her new cream suit would be covered in cat fur if she sat down. There was nowhere else to sit. "I won't sit down, thank you," she said lightly, and told another white lie. "I'd be happy to share my seat but I'm allergic to cats."

"Allergic tae cats!" Mrs. Currie laughed. "Fluffy wouldnae hurt a fly!"

"Och, you canna drink your tea standing up!" said Mrs. McDougal. "Dolly, put Fluffy off."

Mrs. Finlay rumbled with laughter and Ann realized that the guffaw she'd heard earlier came not from a man but from this garishly dressed creature. The woman lifted the still-sleeping cat, which hung like a limp black bow before she rearranged it on her knee.

A thin black snowfall of cat hairs covered the vacated seat. Concerned for her suit and somewhat annoyed by the old women's amusement — there was nothing funny about allergies — Ann sat down and realized that a sickly sweet smell was travelling from Mrs. Finlay. Cheap perfume? Booze? The armchair seat was too close to the floor and she found herself wearing her knees ridiculously near her chin. Oh God, were there fleas?

"D'you like your tea weak or strong, dearie?" asked Mrs. McDougal, teapot poised.

"None, thank you. I've got a little bit of a headache."

"Well then, dearie, all the more reason you should have a cuppa. It opens the veins," Mrs. McDougal said incomprehensibly, and filled the teacup. "Milk and sugar, dearie?"

"I didn't ... oh well, just a little sugar, please," Ann said, and watched while Mrs. McDougal ladled two teaspoonfuls of sugar into the cup. God, she thought. As the other woman stirred vigorously, Ann flashed an appraising glance at the other occupants of the house. Except that her droopy knitted dress was green and she wore butterfly glasses, Nola Currie was a clone of the shabby Mrs. McDougal. The parrot-bright and overly made-up Dolly Finlay, however, was something else. Dolly lived up to her nickname. Shoulder-length earrings shot cheap diamanté fire through ringlets of a fierce metallic blonde; her big feet had been jammed into gold lamé stiletto sandals, one strap of which had been removed to allow room for a bunion. Silver nylons encased muscular legs snaking with varicose veins that disappeared under a scarlet miniskirt, while the low-necked black satin blouse revealed an ancient cleavage as furrowed as a ploughed field. Barbie, Ann thought, one hundred years old.

"Milk, dearie?" Mrs. McDougal was asking. "Seed cake? It's Nola's best. It was her turn tae bake."

"No milk," Ann said, accepting the thick white cup and chipped saucer. "And no cake, thank you, I really don't have the time. My, Mrs. McDougal," she added politely, "you have so many interesting antiques." As she took a sip of tea — too hot, it burned her lips — she slid a glance at the creature to her left.

It was disconcerting to see Mrs. Finlay grinning at her, as if she had read Ann's unspoken opinion and found it amusing. Under the wrinkled lids, livid with iridescent purple eyeshadow, eyes of a startlingly clear and beautiful blue watched Ann in... surely not derision? It gave Ann quite a turn.

"Och, you girls nowadays! I hope you don't believe in that slimming nonsense," Mrs. Currie's lilting voice was commenting.

"'Course she believes in it! Look at her. Skinny as a rake," Mrs. Finlay boomed, lifting a teacup to her lips. A broad gold wedding band winked in the thin sunlight.

If Dolly Finlay sang in a choir, it would be as a baritone, Ann thought. Somewhat embarrassed — she truly had not meant to reveal her opinion of the creature beside her — but annoyed that these old biddies would call her a girl and comment on her personal appearance, Ann murmured, "Hardly a girl. I'll be thirty-six next June." These old women were not what she'd expected: they seemed extraordinarily cheerful, given their obvious poverty. Bet they're on welfare, she thought, just like Dad, content to sit on his butt and pick up a cheque every month.

"Thirty-five ... och, ye're just a bairn!" Mrs. Finlay drawled.

Ann took a sip of tea and hurried to open her briefcase, placing her laptop on the table while she searched for the tin containing the shortbreads. She placed the tin on the table and tried to ignore the throbbing behind her right eye. "I can only stay a minute," she repeated. "I've a lot of work to catch up with at home."

"What a marvel it is," Mrs. McDougal said, touching the laptop. "Would you mind plugging it in, dearie, and let us be having a wee look? There's a plug behind you. Anything technical scares me stiff."

Mrs. Currie said. "Me too, Aggie. Och, I'm glad they didnae have those things when I was a young lass."

More delay. Hiding her impatience, Ann said, "I don't need to plug it in. And there's absolutely nothing to be afraid of." Their generation and mine are so far apart we're like two different species, she thought.

"Well, show us what you can do," Mrs. Finlay boomed.

Was there a sneer in the creature's voice? Nettled, Ann opened Microsoft Word and then clicked on File. "See that list of titles? I can go into any file I want, call up a document, work on it, then close it down and open another document. That's all there is to it." She moved the mouse, preparatory to switching off.

"Och, I just couldnae do that," Mrs. McDougal said.

Ann had heard the same defeatist talk from her sisters when she'd told them of her recent promotion. "You could if you really wanted to," she said.

Mrs. McDougal's colour rose. She stammered, "If you say so, dearie."

She had been too sharp. Her counsellor had told her that her brusque manner had a lot to do with her childhood and the fact that she'd had to bring up her siblings herself, her mother always being too busy with the latest baby. Her migraine was increasing.

"And that's it, that's all?" Mrs. Finlay asked.

"Yes, that's it," Ann lied.

"Can you get the Internet?" Mrs. Finlay asked, leaning to look.

"No," Ann lied. Once they got on the Internet she'd never get them off. Mrs. Finlay, she could tell, didn't believe her, but what the hell, she was entitled to go home, take some Tylenol and put her feet up. Anyway, if they really wanted to learn about such things, there would be free lessons for seniors at their local library.

Her movements had woken the cat. A small triangular head lifted from Mrs. Finlay's knees, slanting green eyes focused on the mouse, and as Ann made the final click, the animal uncoiled with the speed of a snake about to strike. Ann slapped the laptop shut and pushed it into her briefcase. She didn't like cats. That sudden contraction and expansion of the pupil, allowing a glimpse into a blackly murderous world. Unlike dogs, cats were unbiddable.

"Did you say you'd baked the shortbreads, dearie?" Mrs. Currie was asking as she opened the tin. She held it out to Ann.

"Nothing to eat, thank you," Ann said, then burst out laughing. The image of herself slaving over a hot stove was just too far out. "Margaret made them," she said, pressing her fingers against her temple. "I don't bake."

"You can't cook?" Mrs. Finlay asked lazily.

Ann thought of the thousands of cheap meals she'd been forced to prepare while she was growing up. "These days, thank God, a woman doesn't have to cook." What was it about this old biddy with the peculiarly knowing eyes that made her feel six years old again?

"Drink your tea, dearie, or it'll get cold," Mrs. McDougal said.

"Can't cook? So you're not married then?" Mrs. Currie queried. "Are you divorced, then?"

Oh God, Ann thought, here we go. I'm head of a finance department, I own my own condo and all I get is, what, you're not married? "Maybe I'm married to my job," she said, trying to keep her tone light as she replaced the laptop in her briefcase.

Mrs. Finlay's baritone began, "But if you're afraid to try ..."

"I'm not afraid of anything," Ann cut in. And now she felt real resentment at the personal questions and the narrow horizons of these prying old women. She and they had nothing in common, and she was wasting precious time. "It's just not part of my life plan," she added.

"Life plans you, you don't plan it," came Mrs. Finlay's deep guffaw. "O' course, some girls don't want to risk real life. They just want to be —"

"But don't you have a sweetheart?" Mrs. Currie insisted.

"— men in high heels," Mrs. Finlay finished. To Ann's consternation, the old woman suddenly rose and held out her arms to an invisible partner. Trailing her overpowering scent, she strode across the floor, humming what Ann thought was the old song "Jealousy." The creature was performing some sort of tango, diamanté earrings flashing, scarlet miniskirt revealing the full hideousness of her knotty leg muscles with their varicose veins bunching like grapes, the V of her blouse gaping to reveal wrinkled breasts. As the deep grating hum continued from the ruined throat, her two friends began laughing so uproariously that tears ran down their cheeks. Ann felt her gorge rising.

"Och, she's such a card!" Mrs. McDougal spluttered at last, wiping her eyes as Mrs. Finlay sashayed back to her seat. "I'm telling you, dearie, if you don't laugh, you cry. And you're not drinking your tea."

"I'm afraid I really do have to go."

"Next time you mustn't rush away, you must visit us properly," Mrs. McDougal said. "Come by next Tuesday, dearie. It's my turn tae make the sponge cake."

"Thank you," Ann said quickly, "but actually I'm never in this area. I'm only delivering the cookies for Margaret."

Even as the white lie left her mouth, she remembered that she'd already told them she passed this street every day. She could have bitten her tongue off.

Mrs. McDougal flushed a brilliant scarlet. For what felt like an age everyone was silent, then Mrs. Currie said with an obvious effort, "Well now, you said you had a sweetheart?"

Avoiding their eyes, Ann said, "A partner, yes," knowing that this ancient trio would probably call that "living in sin." "And now I really must go," she added.

"But children?" Mrs. McDougal queried. "What about bairns? Don't you want any?"

Another irritant. Old biddies like these failed to understand that many career women nowadays chose not to have children.

"Motherhood is not for me," she said firmly. She could've said, "I've already brought up seven children, thank you," but did not.

The nauseous mixture of cheap scent and damp and cat urine had doubled the pounding behind her eye. "I could never stay home with only children for company," she said, "even if it were only part-time." Pushing the cup and saucer towards the centre of the table as an indication that the visit was over, she said rather too loudly, "I've got my master's in business administration. I enjoy using my mind."

"Using your mind?" Mrs. Finlay interrupted, surfing forward on a wave of scent as she helped herself to a cookie. "You business mistresses nowadays are popping off with heart attacks at fifty, not like us old biddies. Where's the sense in that?"

Disconcerted that this hideous old creature seemed to be mirroring her thoughts back to her, Ann bent over her briefcase and pretended to fiddle with the lock. What had these old women to show for their lives? Probably the same as her grandmother, mother and sisters: one man each, endless pregnancies, endless drudgery, endless juggling to make ends meet.

Mrs. McDougal said, "Och, no need to be afraid o' motherhood, it's all very natural, dearie."

"Excuse me, I said I'm not afraid of anything," Ann said, too exasperated and tired now to care about her tone. She could have told them that she had hitchhiked alone around Europe, gone bungee jumping ... she grabbed the chair arms, indicating that she was about to leave, and said, "I enjoy a challenge and hope to achieve something worthwhile, that's all. The way I look at it, any female can give birth."

Once again, silence shocked the air. Ann could imagine her counsellor's voice murmuring about belligerence, but she was too fed up to care.

Mrs. Currie broke the tension by leaning to address Mrs. Finlay, which meant that Ann couldn't stand up without knocking into her. "Don't forget, Dolly," she said, "nowadays girls can choose when tae have their families."

"Not like us, eh," Mrs. McDougal piped. "Two bairns and one mistake, that's what we used to say."

"Except you ended up with two bairns and five mistakes," Mrs. Finlay's man's voice chortled.

The trio rocked and rolled with laughter.

I've had it, Ann thought, bending forward to indicate that she wanted to stand up. Her stomach knotted as a memory jabbed at her — a thick sweet-sourness, breast milk and shitty diapers. Mother and two of her mother's friends, the three of them so larded with fat after giving birth that one month later they were still in maternity tops. They had been sharing a joke in Grandma's farm kitchen, incomprehensibly cheerful amidst the poverty that was endemic among seasonal workers, and one friend had carelessly bared a breast and thrust a workmanlike red teat into the mouth of her infant. No glossy Playboy sexiness in that scenario. The baby's cheeks working rhythmically as breast milk ran down its chin; her own mother not caring that two large wet circular stains were darkening the front of her maternity top. Through the open window, the grunts and squeals of a dozen piglets fighting in the stinking pigpen for the teats of the sow.

Mrs. Currie seemed not to realize that she was blocking Ann's way. "It's been delightful, but I really must go now," Ann said louder, pressing again on the chair arms. She caught Mrs. Finlay's knowing sapphire gaze and looked away.

"Your job must be so complicated, dearie," Mrs. McDougal said as she eyed Ann's briefcase.

"But not as complicated as having a baby," Mrs. Finlay said, her jewelled gaze on Ann.

"That's true," Mrs. Currie giggled. "Och, I'll not forget having my Lloyd in that mining shack and me screaming my head off! Thought I was going tae die!"

"What us farmer's wives had tae put up with!" Mrs. Finlay's baritone laughed. "Not a soul tae help you. I'm telling you, I thought my pelvis was being ripped out. I nearly had my Jenny among the cows."

"Panting like a dog during the contractions and the midwife telling me tae haul on the sheet and me hauling till I'd nearly pulled my arms out o' their sockets —"

"And the midwife shouting 'don't push, Mrs. McDougal, don't push or it'll come too quick,' and I couldnae ha' stopped pushing for all the tea in China, an' all that slimy stuff dribbling out o' me."

Ann wanted to stand up but her hands were having difficulty with the arms of the chair. The smells of scent and damp and cat urine were overpowering.

"Had tae have nineteen stitches, I was torn that badly from my you-know-what right tae my anus, all jagged it was, couldn't sit down properly for weeks —"

"Gas an' air supposed tae deaden the agony but it didnae help a damn —"

As the gut-wrenching descriptions continued amidst gales of laughter, Ann's head seemed to loosen and float into the room.

Something had happened to Mrs. McDougal's oil paintings; they were revolving, long-horned Highland cattle swimming after one another around the walls. Ann tried to rise, to say, "I have to go now," but her legs had no strength; the velvet seat was too soft and too low, and she was sinking deeper and deeper into the suffocating red depths.

"Afterbirth like a big piece of liver and Sam buried it in the garden as fertilizer for his runner beans."

The voices with their hideous litany of leaking breasts and torn flesh and blood and violence laughed on and on.

"Oh please," Ann whispered. "Please, stop."

Through waves of nausea she saw the laughing faces turn towards her.

"Och, dearie, you're never going tae be sick?" Mrs. McDougal's lilting voice asked. "It's not the milk, is it, dearie? Is it off?"

Mrs. Finlay boomed, "Once in a blue moon one of those critters would give birth tae a freak. There was a special name for them, what was it … och, I canna remember …"

"Let me help you, dearie, you don't look too good," Mrs. Currie said.

Ann was still trembling when at last she climbed into her Porsche. A heavy cloud had shrouded the sun, plunging the surrounding apartment buildings and the little shabby house into shadow. Somehow, she managed to pin a smile on her face for the benefit of the three women waving goodbye from the garden gate. She started the car, then paused as Mrs. Finlay suddenly opened the gate and sashayed towards her, the scarlet miniskirt riding up her bony thighs, the gold stiletto sandals striking sparks from the road's broken surface.

"I've just remembered what the name was," Mrs. Finlay said, leaning in through the window so that Ann received a full blast of sugary scent. The sapphire eyes were gleaming. "Moon calf. That was it. Moon calf. It means those creatures that don't turn out as Mother Nature intended. Freaks, y' know. Well, thanks for a very interesting conversation." Her right eye closed in a knowing wink. "Bye-bye for now, dearie."

Mrs. Finlay swaggered back to the gate. And as Ann drove away and the migraine took agonizing possession of her right eye, she could see the three old women in her rear view mirror, and the grins on the wrinkled faces were so broad they seemed to light up the street.

SCHEHERAZADE AT NOON

She'll be performing her party piece any minute now, Mary thought, noticing that her sister Kathy was checking her watch. The credit union where Mary worked, and Kathy's delicatessen in West Vancouver, were both closed on Mondays. Once a month for the past few months her sister had been inviting new customers — as a rule, middle-aged homemakers whose husbands had been transferred to Vancouver — to a luncheon where they could meet women as lonely as themselves. Trouble is, Mary told herself, eyeing the rotating balloons that constituted Kathy's bum, both the party piece and Kathy's weight are reaching gargantuan proportions.

A minute later, Kathy cried, "Girls, have I got a story to tell you!" Her new purple silk caftan billowed like a galleon under full sail as she moved towards the buffet. She had also tinted her shoulder-length brown hair a silver-gilt shade that had the unfortunate effect of drawing attention to her many chins. For God's sake, Mary thought, watching Kathy pile a plate high with langues de chats — fruit- and cream-filled cookie cups formed from baked egg-white batter — I've just finished telling you your weight is a health problem and look at you! Might as well have kept my mouth shut!

Balancing the laden plate, Kathy returned to her rattan chair, which had a high curving back that lent it a throne-like air. It squealed as she let loose her thighs over the seat. Using the fleshy mass of her knees as a table, she addressed the newcomers. "This story is about Elizabeth O'Grady, girls, the famous actress on *Late Night Challenge*. Before she became famous she used to live right around the corner here."

"You told us that story last time," Queenie Chang said, eyeing Kathy's plate.

"And the time before that," said Cuddles McCormack.

"But there are new people here who haven't heard it," Kathy said firmly.

About fifteen women were either sitting on chairs or on the new needle-pointed cushions scattered about the recently installed pink broadloom, their dessert plates and glasses of white wine beside them. A movement caught Mary's eye. One of the newcomers — Mary had been in the washroom and had missed the introduction — had stood up and was leaning back against a wall, her arms folded as her gaze moved slowly over the crowd. Short black hair cupped her head like a satiny black tulip and her elegant black leather pantsuit stood out against the other women's more casual pastel dresses or pants. Mary noticed a university pin in one of the lapels.

"Well, girls, shall I begin?"

Yes, please get the luncheon over with and then let you and me go to the library, Mary thought. Once again, she was torn between exasperation and concern, for she had just glimpsed her sister's white neck marshmallowed in fat. Kathy's appetite seemed uncontrollable. She was also in some sort of financial mess, which was a surprise, because the delicatessen was doing well. But there we are, Mary thought. If she won't confide in me, I can't help her.

"Let me begin by saying," Kathy said, her hand dithering over langues de chat, "that Elizabeth is beautiful but criminally sly." The biggest langue won.

"Really? I didn't know that," someone said, while the puzzled frowns of Queenie and Cuddles indicated that this bit of scandal was also new to them.

Mary protested, "Criminally sly, Kathy? Last month she was just sly."

Red Morrison's auburn hair disappeared into the kitchen, perhaps because she had heard the story several times already, but Queenie and Cuddles chose to remain. These middle-aged widows, Mary suspected, secretly enjoyed Kathy's repeat performances. Why watch *All My Children* in the loneliness of a bachelor apartment when you can watch the equivalent at Kathy's and meet women as isolated as yourself?

Ignoring Mary, Kathy confided, "You see, girls, Elizabeth knew the secret that makes one person totally irresistible to another.

And that's how she was able to get Sean O'Grady to marry her, right? He used to be Billy Biggs but then he changed it to Sean O'Grady as a special favour to Elizabeth when he saw she was becoming famous."

Yes, thought Mary, an opportunist if ever there was one. Several newcomers, she noticed, were eyeing with disbelief the high-rise that was Kathy's plate.

"In fact, those paintings above the buffet are some of his studies of the female form," Kathy continued. "He's a real professional."

Professional womanizer you mean, Mary thought, staring at the slap and tickle of Sean O'Grady's salmon-coloured nudes. She remembered an affair he'd had with a friend of hers. "He certainly was professional at extracting thousands from a friend of mine," she couldn't resist saying loudly. "She says he's never repaid her."

Kathy's dark eyes burned and she snapped, "Is it Sean's fault if women give him gifts and then turn nasty when the affair's over? Mary is a GCA, girls."

"That's CGA," said Mary.

"Which is why everything has to be weighed and measured. And she's going through a divorce, so I guess that's why she's anti-men right now. Okay girls, let me begin ..."

Now that's a damn low blow, Mary fumed to herself, turning to stare out of the window so that nobody would notice her hot cheeks. Her sister's ground-floor condominium overlooked the road that wound up Hollyburn Mountain to the latest subdivision, and Mary allowed her gaze to linger, as if she were interested in the distant red-tiled roofs semaphoring their sky-high prices through the branches of the few ancient Douglas firs remaining on-site. She thought: why don't I leave now? The library's only a five-minute drive away.

"No beautiful woman," Kathy was saying, "no beautiful woman can accept being dumped. So when Sean found somebody else, Elizabeth decided to write him a very clever letter, because that sly creature was very well aware that there's more than one way of scratching another woman's eyes out."

"How do you know all this?" the black-haired woman interrupted.

"Sean showed me the letter himself, Susan. He trusts me as if I were his sister." Placing her plate on the floor, Kathy heaved herself up and struck a melodramatic pose. "My own darling Sean," she whined. "I don't want to live if you don't love me any more. I've bought some pills and I'm going into the bush to end it all. Goodbye for ever, your Bunty."

Newcomers always fell to pieces when this particular bombshell landed and, except for Susan, today's newcomers were no exception. As for the label "Bunty," up until now the actress had always been referred to as "Elizabeth." From the raised eyebrows of a couple of women, Mary knew that this nickname was new to them, too.

Shock had caused newcomer Toots Labrocca's eyeglasses to slide towards the end of her nose. "You mean," she gasped, adjusting her glasses, "that Elizabeth O'Grady actually attempted suicide?"

"By hook or by crook, she was going to get him," Kathy sang, rolling her eyes. She sat down again and placed her plate on her knees.

"You know, I'm not sure we should be talking like this," an

older woman said suddenly. Mary recognized her as a home-maker from last month's luncheon. "We don't know what really happened."

Right on, Mary thought, smiling encouragingly at her. You tell her! She takes no notice of me.

"Excuse me, I do know because I got it from Sean himself," Kathy snapped.

"When Elizabeth was on TV recently," Mary felt compelled to mention, "she said that everyone does stupid things that they later regret."

"Oh, Bunty isn't stupid," Kathy cut in, her angry gaze flaming towards Mary, "Bunty is criminally sly. I'm telling you, when she comes into the shop, no way will I serve her! I let Julie do it. Just take this pet name she uses all the time. The cuddlesy-wuddlesy bunny-wabbit wiv duh liddle pink nose?" Her tone changed and she added briskly, "Adopting a helpless sounding, childish nick-name is a common trick used by unscrupulous women who don't want the boyfriend knowing that their little sex kitten actually has fangs ten feet long and claws to match."

Breathless after this long speech, she had to come up for air. Queenie and Cuddles were exchanging uncomfortable glances and Mary suffered equal amounts of exasperation and despair.

The woman who had objected suddenly scrambled to her feet and stared at her wristwatch. "Is that the time!" she cried, a little too loudly. "I'm so sorry, Kathy, but I really have to fly! Thank you so much for the delicious lunch."

"Me too," another woman said quickly. "Sunrise Upholstery said they'd send an estimator and I promised I'd be in for them."

See, Kathy? Mary tried telegraphing to her sister as the two women hurried out of the room. You're turning people off.

"Ms. O'Grady," Susan said and then paused while she adjusted the university pin in her lapel. "Ms. O'Grady," she repeated, giving the pin a final pat, "was in my office last week. She's bought in that new subdivision up the road here. She introduced herself as 'Elizabeth,' not 'Bunty.'"

Sounds as if Susan's in the real estate business, Mary thought. As usual, her sister had chosen to ignore any controversial comment. Gaze widening on the bloated breasts of Sean O'Grady's nudes, she cried, "Then, when she'd finished writing the letter, Bunty taped it to the microwave so that Sean would see it when he reheated his favourite dish — English steak and kidney pie — that she'd made for him. Carefully, she reread the wording —"

"She reread the letter? How do you know that?"

"Susan! Let Kathy speak!" Toots broke in.

"I know because Elizabeth is a bad speller. Sean told me so. So she'd have to reread it to check the spelling, right?" Kathy nagged.

This innovation, Mary remembered, had been added last month or had it been the month before? Kathy's mocking gaze was hopping over her audience and she smirked, "Luckily for our Bunty-poo, the weather was fine, for she'd planned her action for the full moon. All was ready, steak and kidney pie in the fridge, fresh-baked cookies in the cookie jar, furniture polished, pink carpets vacuumed. Alongside Sean's chair were the slippers she had needle-pointed for his birthday ..."

It's worse than ever, Mary thought. Her mouth opened to protest but Susan got there before her with, "Oh, so Ms. O'Grady is a good cook and housekeeper and can embroider as well?"

"Susan!" chorused a couple of voices. "Let Kathy tell the story!"

Kathy's stare flayed the young woman before she cried, "What Bunty was really saying was, 'See? These are the home comforts you'll have to do without if you dare to leave me!' Okay, Susan? Anyway, any idiot can embroider! I myself have just finished needle-pointing those cushions there on the floor."

"Are you," asked Susan with a dangerous smile, "telling us that you're an idiot?"

What is this, the third degree? Mary thought, stiffening. It's all right for me to say something to her but you're not her sister.

"Please, no more interruptions!" Kathy insisted. "Now, where was I? Did I say she had already placed juice and pills inside a backpack? And did I say that the moon had turned night into day? All right, there she is, humping the backpack up on her shoulders and clickety-clacking those high heels of hers up the moonlit road —"

"Ms. O'Grady proposed going into the bush at night, wearing high heels?"

"Susan," cried Toots, "for pity's sake!"

"What else was Ms. O'Grady wearing?" Susan pressed, unfolding her arms.

"Pardon? Oh! Cream-coloured silk pants and a cream silk blouse —"

"High heels and cream-coloured silk for tramping through the bush at night?"

Kathy's eyes rolled. "Susan, we're talking West Vancouver! Supposing halfway up the road our Bunty-poo had met a movie producer out for an evening stroll, it would've been bye-bye fake suicide attempt right there and then, I'm telling you!"

Mary saw another woman glance at her watch. Her sister saw it too, and hurried on with, "Anyway, she reached the end of the road. For God's sake gimmee a drink, it's hot in here! Where was I?"

Susan said smoothly, "You had reached the end of the road."

Mary tried catching Susan's eye, wanting the young woman to realize that she shouldn't take Kathy seriously; however, Susan's alert gaze remained on Kathy's flushed face.

"And from there," Kathy cried, "there was nothing but wilderness stretching into infinity."

This stupid story must be six months old by now, Mary thought. We should buy a cake, decorate it with six candles and sing "Happy Birthday."

"Now, although Bunty had taken all the steps necessary for faking a suicide —"

"Oh, Kathy!" Mary couldn't help groaning.

"A fake suicide," Mary insisted. "But of course no one guessed that, least of all poor Sean."

"What a bitch that Elizabeth O'Grady sounds," Toots murmured.

"Oh, our Bunty," smirked Kathy, "is an absolute cow."

"But surely, if Ms. O'Grady were only faking suicide," Susan drawled, shifting position against the wall and re-folding her arms (Mary got the impression of a black hawk rearranging its wings) "she would've chosen a motel, not the bush. Too dangerous."

"Don't forget she's criminally sly and wanted it to look real, eh?" Kathy said. "Anyway, Bunty hadn't decided where to perform her big act. She wanted a place where she'd be unconscious when the police found her, but not so far away that they wouldn't find her until she was a goner. Soon, those silver-gilt curls of hers were wet and bedraggled ..."

"How do you know that?"

"And her clothing was smeared!" Kathy cried, loud enough to drown Susan out. "At last, she came to a rocky clearing — as a matter of fact, girls, it's where that new subdivision's going up right now — with one of those big hollow cedar stumps in the centre. Fallen branches had given it a kind of roof. Bunty clicked her high heels towards the stump, and then she made herself comfortable. Humming to herself, she checked her nails and then took makeup and a hairbrush out of her backpack ..."

Where the hell, Mary asked herself, does Kathy dig up this crap?

"Humming?" Susan queried. "And she checked her nails and redid her makeup? Where's the proof?"

Kathy's pudgy hand dimpled as she smoothed back her new blonde curls. Dubious eyes had swivelled towards her, their owners awaiting the proof, now that someone had mentioned the matter. Placing her laden plate on the floor once more, as if Susan's constant questioning had put her off her food, Kathy avoided Mary's exasperated stare and explained with weary patience, "The proof is that I've studied that woman and I know every thought that goes on in that sly blonde head, oh yes! If by some terrible accident Bunty did die, she wanted an elegant corpse, right? So much more appealing than a corpse in baggy jamaicas and stinky old sneakers, right? And she's also a singer, right? Of course she hummed ..." Kathy paused as a woman on the outskirts of the group raised a hand in apologetic farewell before tiptoeing out. "So there's Bunty," Kathy continued quickly, "humming to herself, redoing those glistening nails of hers and touching up her lipstick, polishing and preening and brushing her silver-gilt curls until they gleamed in the moonlight. Her lips were pink and moist against the creamy velvet of her complexion, her eyes shone with that peculiar cold gold of hers."

I give up, Mary thought. Even those who had been listening willingly now looked dubious about such minutiae, and Kathy, obviously reading their minds, nagged, "Because Bunty-poo always tarts herself up to look like a dog's dinner! Wouldn't you want to look your best if you were trying to out-do another woman?"

And Mary, hoping that her sister's act would soon be over, wondered if at some point in other apartments in other cities, some of these women would look at their husbands and agree that yes, this is what rival women do to each other; or maybe, years hence, they would remember when they, too, had once feared another woman, and they would recall the anguish and the prayers and the tears, and would wish that they could have that pain back just one more time, so that they could know they were still capable of feeling something, anything.

The familiar words were rolling along their well-worn tracks. "Then she fished inside her backpack," Kathy was saying, "and took out the juice and pills. Sean told me later that Bunty had actually swallowed the first pill, but I know that woman, oh yes! She was waiting for the police to come racing up as she was struggling — oh so despairingly, of course — to unscrew the lid with those long gleaming nails of hers, and the police shouting, 'For God's sake, Ma'am, don't do it!' and them grabbing the bottles and her bursting into tears ... and people say this woman is beautiful but dumb?"

"You said beautiful but criminally sly," murmured Susan.

"Beautiful but criminally sly, beautiful but dumb, it's all the same! However, Bunty didn't get a chance to go into her big act, because that was the very moment when ..." And Kathy paused, raising her eyebrows and staring around at the assembled women.

I cannot listen to this rubbish for one minute longer, Mary thought, and slipped into the kitchen to join Red Morrison. Red ran her own hairdressing business and was finishing stacking her business cards on a shelf before turning to pile plates into the dishwasher. Through the open doorway Mary saw Toots urge, "That was the very moment when what?" Red's jaw was moving and Mary realized that the other woman was mimicking in unison with Kathy: "Because that was the very moment when Elizabeth O'Grady ... met ... her match."

You bitch, Mary thought, glaring at Red's navy silk-clad back as she bent over the dishwasher, grabbing yourself a high class free meal while drumming up business! How many clients have you obtained so far, eh, thanks to my sister? Her gaze burned towards the women gathered in the living room. And that's true for a few others, too, she thought. Coming here to be wined and dined, using my sister's condo as a club — you don't give a damn about Kathy. Bet you rip her character to shreds the minute you're out of here. Then her anger changed to helplessness. It was Kathy's choice to put on this god-awful show. How many of the newcomers could guess that Kathy had been the type of child who would rescue drowning worms, that she had baked Granddad a cake every Sunday after he'd lost Grandma, that she had been a pleasure to be with until the black day she met Billy Biggs a.k.a. Sean O'Grady.

Her sister had started pacing up and down, hands gesturing as her caftan flapped about her legs. "Bunty told Sean that she had been looking at the sky, saying goodbye to life — can you believe such claptrap, girls — and when she looked down, she thought her eyes hadn't adjusted properly to the moonlight because the nearby bushes had changed colour." Kathy halted, screwed her eyes up tight and then chanted, "Elizabeth closed her eyes, opened them and then she realized that she was looking at ... a cougar."

"My God, a cougar!"

Always, at this point, came this excitation of breath and babble and bangles. Even those women who had been listening with pursed lips now looked frightened. Every gaze was fastened on Kathy's vivid face, and Red had stopped stacking dishes in order to watch. Susan was the only woman who seemed outside the general audience, her slim black figure motionless against the wall.

Hands clasped to her bosom in the manner of the early movie heroines, Kathy whispered, "This is what Elizabeth told Sean, word for word, I swear it to God. All the muscles in her body bunched up, ready to flee. The cougar stood motionless, a gleaming statue in the moonlight, its steady gaze levelled straight at her. Then it lifted its shining head and sniffed the air. It paced forward, and Bunty saw a hump rising between massive gleaming shoulder blades, and powerful legs with huge paws ending in long, terrible claws." And now Kathy's eyes narrowed and her voice dropped to a penetrating whisper. "The cougar paused to test the air again, and then it flowed forward, yes, flowed, for its movement was smoother than pouring cream. This time, its belly was only inches above the ground."

As had happened during previous storytellings, several heads in today's semicircle shrank into Laura Ashley and Edward Chapman necklines; the leg muscles above the Magli ankle straps and Gucci flatties tightened. Ignoring Susan's motionless figure, Kathy cried to the semicircle, "Then Bunty whirled and clawed her way into the stump!" Mary had a clear view of bunching leg muscles and knew that those muscles were flinging their owners into the hollow tree stump along with Elizabeth O'Grady.

"She didn't hear her pants rip as the cougar's claws reached her," sang Kathy into the electric air. "She felt only the agony that ignited on her right leg, heard only the roars of the cougar exploding around her. Knees jammed against her chin, she saw the cougar's silver-gilt head with its glistening fangs flashing only inches from her face, and she fought back blindly, screaming and screaming, beating and beating with a broken branch at the thunder and tumult trying to smash apart the stump."

One woman had started to fidget, but sheer terror distorted the faces of the three newcomers sitting at Kathy's feet. For these three, Mary knew, frail twigs were snapping in their nerveless fingers, they were drowning in the hot, meaty smell of cougar, flowing out of the stump and up into those great slavering jaws.

"The cougar fell back," panted Kathy, beginning to pace again. "One second, two seconds, three seconds, and then it charged. Space exploded around Bunty, and again she thrashed and thrashed with the branch! Her bones and bloodied flesh were trembling with such violence that the branch danced between her fingers;

her own lips were drawn back in a snarl as she fought to save her-self. One second, two seconds, three seconds, then a tornado hit the stump and the cougar got its head inside before the branch caught it in one eye and it fell back. My God, I need a drink!"

Oh yes, Mary thought, watching the newcomers' faces as Kathy poured herself more wine, those three are dying, their flesh is bubbling crimson and there is no God in all the world.

"You should go on the stage yourself," she burst out, and was punished by a glare as her sister drank deep. The woman who had been fidgeting, however, grinned. Then Mary saw Susan bend down, lift her purse, tiptoe towards the bathroom, and just before she closed the door, take something out of her purse. A cell phone? Offering to show a house to a client, Mary thought, and why not, we're all wasting our time here. Kathy hadn't noticed. Her big breasts were heaving as she emptied the glass. She had, however, noticed the enthralled listeners in front of her. Concentrating on these three, she tore them apart with, "The cougar began to pace around the stump. Her breath rattling, the branch feverish between her fingers, Bunty listened to the cougar's long claws clicking across the rock. The animal moved regularly past the stump opening, and each time Bunty's muscles knotted together, and each time the cougar moved its gleaming body past her vision and click, click, clicked across the rock." Kathy clicked her nails down the arm of her rattan armchair.

"Oh! Ohh! Ohhh!"

Kathy crooned, "The clicking ceased. Bunty waited, moan-ing. Then she heard coarse breathing overhead. She looked up, and in the clear moonlight saw the cougar staring down at her through the fallen branches. Numbly, she noted the gleaming velvet of the facial fur, the pink, moist shine of its open jaws, the burning ice of its golden gaze. Then it lowered a paw and began to fish the air, all the while paralyzing her in the fire and ice of its golden eyes." Kathy's low voice swooped to high do and she chanted, "Bunty's bones forgot all meaning at the sight of that terrible beauty, and she dissolved and waited docilely for death."

Toots turned to stare unseeingly at Susan as that young woman left the bathroom and resumed her position against the wall. As was usual at this point, a couple of women were wet-eyed. Inevitably, someone would blow her nose, and this time it was widowed Fran Lee, a gentle Asian woman who had attended the luncheon last month and who obviously hadn't yet adjusted to the tempo of it all.

Kathy waited until the delicate trumpeting had ceased and then she continued, "Presently, the cougar realised that it couldn't fish Bunty up. Once again the cold, golden eyes inspected her, then they withdrew. Bunty heard a thud, then the click, click, click as the cougar padded towards the entrance of the stump. It sat down and began to groom itself, polishing and preening until its fur shone in the moonlight. And presently, Bunty heard a grating noise. It was purring. Bunty trembled in the tree stump and the cougar hummed happily on the rock, and at last, it rolled over on its back, paws flapping, its smooth belly revealing it to be a ...?"

"Female?" whispered Toots, one trembling hand steadying her eyeglasses.

"What else but female!" cried Kathy. "Then it rolled on to its feet and got back to business. And so in this manner the cougar entertained herself all night, and at dawn, she yawned, and stretched, and slipped quietly away."

You won't have long to wait now, Mary thought, glancing at Susan's impassive face, and from her to the restless outer circle of women; Kathy's nearly finished.

Kathy had bowed her head but raised it to say softly, as if the cougar might overhear, realize its mistake and come charging back again in order to finish Elizabeth off, "It was hours before Bunty had the courage to flee down the mountain. Sean told me he found her stumbling up their driveway, covered in blood. And guess what? That was the first Sean knew of her fake suicide attempt, because he hadn't noticed the letter she'd taped to the microwave. He'd eaten the pie straight from the fridge, congealed fat and all, and assumed she was spending the night at her mother's. And do you know what he told me? I'll never forget it as long as I live." Something seemed to catch in Kathy's throat and after a pause she continued huskily, "He told me, 'I can't leave her now, Kathy. I never dreamed any woman would rather die than live without me.'" She swallowed, paused, then said in normal tones, "You see, girls, Bunty had discovered the secret that makes one person totally irresistible to another. The ultimate compliment. Dying for love. Romeo and Juliet. They flew to Reno and were married that very night."

Kathy bowed her head, silent at last.

Half-hearted clapping rose from the women in the outer circle, while the clapping of the trio in front was loud and enthusiastic. Toots exclaimed, "My God, what a story! And it's all true!"

"All something, anyway," Red said, too busy collecting her business cards to realize she had spoken aloud.

Thank God, Mary thought, the show's over. Women were inviting one another to visit, politely declining second helpings of dessert, and in some cases, third helpings, as they began sorting out sweaters and jackets. Susan, she noticed, was smilingly asking a couple of women for their telephone numbers and writing the numbers in a notebook. Future clients, she told herself.

Pushing a handkerchief around her steamed-up glasses, Toots told Kathy, "French cooking is yummy, but all that butter and cream sure loads on the pounds."

"I don't care about that," Kathy said, flopping into the rattan chair.

"Oh, I wasn't thinking about your figure. I was thinking about your health. Your heart."

Kathy said in a low voice, "I don't care about that, either."

Queenie Chang queried, "Didn't I read that Elizabeth divorced that Sean almost immediately?"

"Oh yes, she found some excuse or other," Kathy said. Now that the performance was over, she looked drained. "But another woman got her claws into him immediately. Women just won't leave him alone. However, he's always stayed best friends with me. He says I'm special." Kathy turned her head and for a few seconds Mary was able to look directly into her eyes. Her sister's face was an open wound.

Oh my God, Mary told herself, Kathy's crazily in love with that rotten creep! And I bet she's supporting the bastard too, she thought with sudden insight. That's why she's in a financial mess. Why didn't I see all this before? I should've guessed.

She was worrying how best to help her sister when Susan

entered the kitchen, notebook in one hand, briefcase in the other. Red was just leaving. Pausing to tuck the notebook inside her briefcase, Susan asked mildly, "Does Kathy often tell that story about Elizabeth O'Grady faking suicide?"

Red remained silent. "What?" Mary asked. "Why do you ask?"

"Just curious. Does she?"

To Mary's surprise, Red answered, "No, she never does."

Susan said, "Really? I gathered that Kathy tells this story whenever she gives a luncheon, which is about once a month, hm? In fact, I got the distinct impression that Kathy is a sort of Scheherazade at noon?"

What's going on here? Mary asked herself. She said, "What has a folk tale to do with Kathy?"

"Nothing," Susan drawled. "After all, it's not a sultan who's cutting a woman to pieces, is it? It's not Kathy who has a knife stuck in her back. Well, it's been very nice meeting everyone. I do hope we'll meet again. Goodbye." Opening the door that led to the parking lot, she left.

"Why did you say Kathy never tells that story?" Mary asked Red. "She won't shut up about the damn thing!"

"I do Susan's hair every week. She's a criminal lawyer and ambitious as all hell."

"What? I thought she was in real estate!"

"You kidding? She's just opened her own office in West Van. Didn't you see her handing out business cards?"

"Oh God! Does Kathy know?" Nervously, Mary turned and saw that her sister was struggling to lever her massive bulk out of her chair.

Suddenly, Mary knew. "Oh, Christ ...!" Dropping the cutlery, she ran out of the kitchen and into the parking lot, crying, "Susan! Susan!"

The lawyer was walking towards a gleaming black Porsche, but halted as Mary ran towards her.

"Susan ... please ... Can't you see what Kathy's doing?"

"What are you talking about?"

"Dying for love!" Mary cried. "The ultimate compliment, remember? She's eating herself to death! What do you mean, Kathy hasn't got a knife stuck into her? That bastard Sean O'Grady is whittling her life away!"

Susan said, "You must excuse me. I've got an important appointment in five minutes."

"For Chrissake, she's very sick! She needs help!"

"Excuse me, please."

Tucking her briefcase firmly under her arm, Susan continued towards her Porsche.

PHOENIX RISING

*T*he interior of the crowded bus reeked of hot oil. Trying to ignore the smell, Phoebe swung her suitcase up on the rack before settling herself in the one remaining window seat. Three hours of discomfort lay ahead before they reached Whistler. Kevin had taken the car when he'd walked out, a fact that the lawyers were supposed to consider when dividing the assets of their forty-two-year-old marriage.

The bus driver had ceased cramming ski equipment into the luggage compartment and was helping someone up the step. A white-haired, overweight woman in a crimson ski suit and matching toque rose into view, her gaze searching the bus. Perhaps because she thought Phoebe was about her own age, the woman told the driver, "Ta, love, there's a seat 'ere," swung a bag on the rack and collapsed beside Phoebe with a loud "Blimey! Thought I'd never make it!"

A Londoner, Phoebe thought, recognizing the cockney accent. She smiled tightly, moving her new black purse out of the way as the woman wiggled her large rear end around in an attempt to get comfortable. The new purse, Phoebe thought, was too glittery. Why was it that the cheaper the purse, the shinier the vinyl and the more extravagant the gold metal trim?

"All right, love?" the woman puffed, dumping her own big purse on her lap. "Not taking up too much room, am I?"

Phoebe became aware of a fruity aroma. Booze at seven o'clock in the morning? "No, it's all right," she lied.

"Only they don't give you much room, do they?" The woman laughed, as if such discomfort were a great joke. Veins like red threads spread from the inner corners of her blue eyes. She had no eyelashes, only a kind of pale stubble.

"No, not much," Phoebe said.

Young people were piling in. Their shouts as they recognized friends and their constant laughter ate at what little energy Phoebe had remaining after the past tumultuous months. She stared through the window at the milling crowds waiting to board the rows of Greyhound buses. Perhaps some of the younger travellers were off to start new lives. That's what I should've done after the kids left home, she thought: upgraded my education and got myself a good career. If I'd done that, I wouldn't be in the mess I'm in now. But then, when girls married forty years ago, they didn't have a career. The house, the kids and the husband were the career.

"Busy, innit?"

"Yes."

And yet, according to Walter Scholta's letter, her old friend Brenda had had a career. Not like she and Val. Brenda, in spite of three children, had worked outside the home, ending up as the financial director of the firm where she'd started as a secretary. And now Brenda, like Val, had passed on. Val had been as poor as Phoebe herself, the two of them staying home, dependent on their husbands for pocket money. All very well if your husband appreciated you. Tom had appreciated Val; Kevin hadn't appreciated Phoebe. Now she was battling him for 50 percent of his pension. Her reward for forty-two years of faithful service was grinding poverty.

The bus shook as the driver slammed shut the luggage compartment. Scrambling into his seat, he began to manipulate the gears. An extra-loud bellow, a spine-wrenching jerk, and then they were rolling towards the station exit. Well, Phoebe thought, this is it.

"All right are you, love?" the Cockney voice asked above the noise. The bloodshot eyes were brightly inquisitive.

"I ... yes, thank you."

"Only you look a bit strained, a bit worried, like."

"It's nothing. I was deep in thought," Phoebe said. And then, because after all the woman was only trying to be friendly, she added, "I was just thinking how virtue doesn't always pay, that's all."

"Blimey, you can say that again!" The woman laughed, yanking off her toque. Twists of white curls exploded like miniature Catherine wheels about her head. "Phew, warm, innit?" She added.

"It is, yes."

Phoebe touched the unfamiliar stiffness of her own newly bronzed and sprayed hair. The stylist was not top quality, but because she worked out of her basement she offered rock-bottom prices. Once again, Phoebe found herself wondering what the years had done to Brenda's looks. Brenda had been so pretty, but her good looks had also been her downfall. That was why Tommy McDougal had pursued her until he'd caught her.

The bus was cutting through side streets. Shoppers wandered the stained sidewalks, moving in and out of stores offering extra-cheap groceries, clothing, china and bedding. One block over, Phoebe had rented an extra-cheap bachelor apartment in an extra-cheap low-rise.

"Dump, innit? Live in Coquitlam, meself, not too bad. Fancy a cuppa?"

The woman was unscrewing a vacuum flask. Laced? Phoebe smiled her refusal, and the woman said confidently, "The name's Millie. What's yours?"

"Phoebe. Mother liked the classics. My ex-husband called me Phoenix when I was younger ..." Her voice trailed away. No point in explaining the love-talk from those early, innocent years.

They were leaving the poorer area behind now and moving into the business district. High-rise office blocks towered.

"Going to Whistler, are you, Phoenix? Or getting off at Squamish?"

"I prefer the name Phoebe. Someone's meeting me at Whistler."

"Whistler's beautiful, eh? Like a Walt Disney movie. Got a daughter working in a hotel there. You're lucky, I tell 'er, living in Fairyland, you are."

"It's certainly very different from Vancouver."

The driver halted to let pedestrians surge over a crosswalk. An office tower of black glass leaned over them, plunging the bus into shadow. For a few frightening, suffocating seconds, Phoebe couldn't get her breath.

"Born in the UK, meself. Left it as soon as I saw they weren't going to let me be Queen," Millie said with a cackling laugh. "There's no virtue in poverty, that's what I say."

"No," Phoebe said.

"No virtue in riches either," Millie spluttered, as if she couldn't get enough of her own joke. "Except at least you get a decent roof over your head while you're busy being unvirtuous!"

"Precisely," said Phoebe. Turning slightly away (she didn't want to be rude) she concentrated on the crowds outside. So many young women, so smartly dressed, so confident looking. Did they still believe in the myth of happy ever after?

Presently they entered the causeway cutting through the green of Stanley Park.

"Seeing your family are you then, Phoenix?"

"Actually, it's Phoebe. No, it's the widower of an old friend of mine."

"Yeah?"

The rising tone was an invitation to provide more information. Phoebe hesitated and then said, "Brenda died of cancer several weeks ago, poor thing. She and I and another friend used to be so close, but then Val and I lost touch with her. Val herself died of cancer last year. She would've been as amazed as I am to find that for many years Brenda had been living only a few miles from us."

"Oh?" Millie's eyes brightened with the avidity of the nosy parker, the type who insists on exchanging life stories with strangers at bus stops or on buses. "How did he know where to contact you, then?"

I should've kept quiet, Phoebe thought. "He found an old address book when he was going through her things, so he sent me a card announcing she'd died. I was shocked."

"So then he asked to meet you, did he?"

"Well, I wrote back some nice things about Brenda and he obviously wants to talk about old times. He's very lonely, you can tell."

They had reached the Lions Gate Bridge, its strings of coloured lights making it a fairy rainbow linking two communities that were exact opposites. At the bridge's northern end lay the afflu- ent suburb of West Vancouver, gateway to the soaring mountains whose snowy peaks were cutting diamond triangles out of a sapphire sky. Already, she could glimpse the large, elegant homes and lovely gardens bright with spring flowers.

Millie had turned and was exchanging light-hearted banter with some teenage boys. Their noisy laughter battered Phoebe's nerves as the bus rolled past the shopping mall of Park Royal.

"Cor, look at them posh dresses. Must be lovely to have money, eh, Phoenix?"

"Phoebe. Yes, I'm sure it is."

Then they were moving up a long hill. Phoebe concentrated on the elegant homes.

"Whadya mean, Phoenix? You wonder what else he's found?"

My God, she must have spoken her thoughts aloud! It was a bad habit she'd fallen into lately in an effort to counteract the silence of her apartment. She couldn't be bothered to correct this deaf old woman yet again. Phoebe said, "I guess there's no harm in telling you, since you never knew them. Forty-eight years ago ..."

She hesitated. Brenda had sworn Val and her to secrecy with all the intensity of a seventeen-year-old's "for ever and ever until you die, so help you God." But then she thought: yes, but Val's gone and now Brenda's gone too. "Forty-eight years ago, when Brenda was a teenager, she had a son by a man who dumped her the minute he learned she was pregnant. I get the feeling ..." The bus had slowed as the driver changed gears; now it jerked forward so violently that she was almost thrown from the seat. "That Walter knows nothing about it," she finished, re-anchoring herself.

At the mention of the child, Millie's eyes and mouth opened into three big Os. "Blimey!" she said. "But what makes you think she never told 'im?"

"He wrote me a long letter," Phoebe said, her gaze on the breathtaking entrance to British Properties with its long green lawns and ornamental cherry trees billowing like a sea of sugary pink foam, so different from her own grassless and treeless area. "He's really hurting, you can tell. And from the way he writes it's pretty obvious he's got no idea she'd had a child. There's a big box of old unmarked photographs, he says, and he'd appreciate my help in identifying them. He's staying with his daughter right now, so I'm guessing he's too lonely to go back to his own house. She's making us dinner and I'm to stay the night."

"Yeah, but you're not going to tell 'im, eh? It was nearly fifty years ago. Let it alone, I would."

They were high up now, turning on to the freeway that cut through West Vancouver. When the freeway reached Horseshoe Bay it would branch off into the narrow road that coiled alongside Howe Sound until it reached Squamish. After that it would be a straight run to Whistler. Phoebe could see the shimmering blue distances of the Georgia Strait, shawled on the horizon by the darker blue of Vancouver Island. Hesitantly, she said, "I was wondering if Brenda would want me to tell —"

"You kidding? If she'd kept quiet all these years? Listen, how old is hubby?"

"I'm guessing around sixty-seven."

"The double standard generation, eh? Keep my mouth shut, love, that's what I'd do. Let sleeping dogs lie."

"Yes, but ..." Phoebe said, beginning the argument that had been with her ever since she had received Walter Scholta's letter. "I remember those days only too well. If an unmarried girl got pregnant, she might as well slit her throat. Brenda had to go into a home for unmarried mothers because her parents were too ashamed to let her stay with them. You know the filthy names that unmarried mothers and their babies were called."

"Whores and bastards. Tell me about it!" Millie said with a peculiar laugh.

"But things have changed so much since then. And Walter mentioned three children. Wouldn't they like to know they have a half-brother somewhere? Aren't they entitled to know? That's what's bothering me. I mean, I can give them the birth date, the name of the church home and the name of the adoption agency if they wanted to trace their brother. And maybe Walter would be delighted to know that there's another part of Brenda still alive and kicking somewhere."

"I dunno," Millie said, the corners of her mouth angling downwards. "What, you're sixty-seven an' you suddenly discover your wife had had a son afore she met you? An' you believing she'd always been as pure as the driven snow? And what about the son, eh? Maybe he won't want nothing to do with it." She paused for a few seconds, then mumbled, "Not all of them do, I'm telling youse."

The houses on this stretch of the road were even bigger and more beautiful than those near the shopping centre. Her gaze lingering on the imposing entrances and massive picture windows, Phoebe said, "But supposing Walter's found something he doesn't understand? Say he's found photos of the baby, or a box or something, with baby clothes in it. She kept the baby for three weeks before the church took it away. And I can tell you ..." She hesitated, because suddenly Brenda's agony was very close.

"Yeah? What?"

"She went through the fire all right. When the matron and the adoptive parents took the baby from her, Brenda fought. Her parents had to hold her back."

"Oh my God!"

They were silent, the image too near, too cruel.

"Queer, innit?" Millie said, and Phoebe thought she heard a wobble in the cockney voice. "A man can be a father a hundred times over an' never know it. But a woman —"

"She never wrote to Val and me after they took the baby away," Phoebe said. "And we'd been close for years. Val never understood why she dropped us, but I did. She had to start all over with a completely new life."

Out of the window Phoebe saw low-rise apartments, all shimmering glass, honey-coloured marble and manicured grounds. An apartment here could knock you back half a million dollars.

"Tell you what, don't say a word unless he asks."

"But what if he's waiting for me to say something?"

"My advice is, keep quiet. If he produces a souvenir of the baby an' asks if you know what it means, go very, very careful-like. Don't say nothing if you sense it would hurt 'im, eh? Do have a cuppa, dear, I got plenty fresh milk in this little carton."

"No, really, I'm fine, thank you."

But the other was carefully pouring tea into a spare thermos top. "Milk?"

"Oh ... well ... a little, please."

"Sugar?"

"Just a quarter of a teaspoonful."

"Bloomin' strict with yourself, aren't you, love? Meself, I pile it on, pile it on."

No suspicious taste flavoured the hot liquid; it was plain, straightforward tea.

"I mean, what's the point of disillusioning 'im, eh?" Millie asked. "It might even turn 'im against your friend's memory. In fact, you can bet your bottom dollar it would turn 'im if he's still one of them double standard silly buggers."

"I know what you're saying," Phoebe said.

There was something else, something she hadn't thought through properly yet. A sense of power. It had arrived with Walter's invitation. For the first time in years, she had felt important; had felt ... yes, powerful. Even queenly. "I am not a bad person," she said suddenly.

"'Course you aren't! The very idea!"

"My husband walked out six months ago and refuses to pay me any support. You think there are laws to protect abandoned wives, and there are, but only on paper. Try getting them enforced! I don't mind telling you I've been through hell. Now I'm trying to make a new life for myself and I don't want to repeat my old mistakes. I'd let myself get too dependent on a man."

"A woman has to do what a woman has to do. You know, dear," Millie confided, "when my Jackie started taking me out regular, that's what he asked me. Was I a virgin? Bloomin' cheek!" She fell back against the seat, her mouth wide with laughter. Phoebe caught a glimpse of gold teeth.

Kevin had asked her the same question. As far as she knew, right up to the Swingin' Sixties all men had asked that question. It was considered their right. Women did not have the same right to demand virginity in their man.

"I told 'im o' course I am!" Millie guffawed. "I knew what side my bread was buttered on! None of his business, anyway, what I'd done afore I met 'im. An' he wasn't a virgin, he'd made damn sure o' that! Well, we all got our little secrets, haven't we?"

"But that's how it was, wasn't it? It's so different now. I don't mind telling you Kevin was the only man I've ever had." Or ever likely to have? an inner voice nagged.

"Are you a virgin, indeed!" Millie repeated on a puff of rich breath. "Fifty happy years I gave 'im, so he had nothing to grumble about. It wouldn't 've been as good if I hadn't had a bit of experience, so he should ha' given thanks to God an' shut up. Look at these houses, my God, you got to be royalty to live 'ere."

The homes in this most westerly part of West Vancouver could qualify as estates. Many of them, Phoebe knew from the real estate printout in her local paper, were valued in the millions. Fiddling in her new purse, she found and removed Walter's photograph. "There he is," she said. "He sent it so I'd recognize him at the bus stop."

"Hmm, got a tight little mouth on 'im," Millie said, holding the photograph close to her eyes. "This his own house in the background?"

"His and Brenda's house, yes. That's their back garden."

"Bloomin' palace, innit? An' that car!"

"Yes," Phoebe said.

"'Course," Millie cackled, "a frog can turn into a prince. An' vice versa."

"Indeed."

"The house can't be far from where we are now," Millie said, pointing at the photograph. "See? That's Cypress Ridge, in the background."

"I thought it was."

Handing back the photograph, Millie said, "Keep in mind he mightn't thank you for telling 'im, if you tell 'im."

"On the other hand he might thank me very much indeed. He might be deeply grateful, forever grateful."

"Well, Phoenix, you got to do the right thing."

"Yes," Phoebe said, "I know."

"I got to have a little bit of kip now. Feel a bit tired, like."

Kip? "Please go ahead."

Pulling on her toque, Millie settled herself. Gradually, the toque slipped down her nose, and after a while, soft gurgles grated in and out of her open mouth. A burst of noisy youthful laughter erupted from the seats alongside. Phoebe stared between the bobbing heads at the magnificent view of Howe Sound and once again thought her thoughts.

As the bus lurched into the square at Whistler, Millie woke up. Phoebe was already on her feet, bending from her height to stare through the window at the wandering groups of people, most of them wearing brightly coloured ski suits.

"Walt Disney, I'm tellin' youse," Millie said, indicating the pink-tinged cobblestones, the gingerbread townhouses with their window boxes overflowing with flowers, the turquoise-roofed hotels disguised as Swiss chalets.

"There he is," Phoebe said. "Oh ... he's a bit shorter than I thought. I shouldn't have worn high heels." Up came her hands to smooth her hair, and then down to smooth her unfashionable navy skirt and jacket and she asked, "Do I look all right? I feel a bit like a beggar maid."

"Don't do it, Phoenix."

"Thank you for your advice. It was very nice talking to you."

"Yeah. Well, good luck, then."

The front and rear doors opened and a pine-scented breeze blew in. Phoebe pushed her way into the crowded aisle, then she was outside and walking towards the eager-faced older man in the elegant grey suit.

BALANCING

The Vancouver Sun lay where Ted had thrown it. Annie switched off the vacuum cleaner and began tidying the pages. Obviously there was nothing in the employment section otherwise Ted would have mentioned it.

She wasn't consciously looking for a promising headline; nevertheless, one caught her eye. It blared, NEIGHBOURS ON WARPATH.

Ted was preparing for his gig and the shower was still running. Tara and Brendan were playing with a ball in the high-rise's parking lot. Quickly, she skimmed the article. A Neil Stevens of Burnaby had upset his neighbours on Dunlop Road by fencing off the land beside his house. Everyone had used it for years as a shortcut to the stores; now, those without cars — including mothers with children — had to make a mile-long detour.

The familiar excitement was stirring. The shower had stopped running and to be on the safe side she called, "H-h-how's it going, Ted?"

Suddenly he was looming in the doorway, naked except for his shorts. Black hair curled over his chest and belly and formed a black sunburst above his crotch. He was holding the telephone bill. "What's this, paying to block call-back? We're supposed to be fucking economizing, stupido!"

"B-b-but dear, it might be someone we owe m-money to."

His belligerent look disappeared and for a moment he looked lost. "God, I can't keep pace. I ..." Then, recovering: "Did you pick up my black shirt?"

"In the closet."

As he turned towards their bedroom she caught sight of the black fuzz on his shoulders and legs. When they were both sixteen and new to sex his male hairiness had turned her on. That's what had got her into trouble, she thought, smoothing back her fair hair she cut herself. She listened to him moving about their bedroom. He would be busy for the next few minutes so she could ... The road map was in the kitchen table drawer. Grabbing the newspaper, she hurried into the kitchen and sat where she could still see her children.

First, the detective work: her wits pitted against the person who had committed an anti-social act; detective work that proved she wasn't as stupid as people might think. She examined the telephone directory and saw that Burnaby had prefixes of 421, 422, 424 and 425. Then she turned to the listings. The name Stevens occupied six columns.

For a while she waited, ears honed for Ted, and then ran her finger down the N. Stevens listings. None of the prefixes matched. This made it more difficult. Either Neil Stevens had an unlisted number, or he used his middle name, and was listed under his first initial. That meant she had to go through all six columns of names, alert for the prefixes. And there he was: J. Neil Stevens, 3516 Dunlop Road, Burnaby.

The excitement was overwhelming. She couldn't wait for Ted to leave. She dialled the number.

And then, just as a male voice said "Hello?" Brendan and Tara raced into the apartment shouting, "Mom! Can we have an ice cream? Mom?"

The voice repeated, "Hello?"

"Mom!"

The Dickie Dee truck was tinkling like the Pied Piper of Hamlin, enticing all children to buy. "Daddy has no money! Go and play!" she hissed, pushing them away with one hand while turning to mutter, "Neil Stevens?"

"Speaking."

Closing the door on her children's pleading, she spat, "I just want you to know what a fucking prick you are."

"What the ... Who the hell are you?"

"Why don't you drop dead, fucking stupido!" She banged the telephone back into its cradle.

Tara and Brendan had returned to the parking lot, their small dark heads drooping as the siren call of Dickie Dee faded. Annie's own disappointment was twofold: being forced to deny her children a treat, and then her anticipated high deflating. Just her luck, to have the kids arrive at the very best moment, when the astonishment and rage of the other person sizzled down the line.

She could smell the petroleum before Ted's belligerent face appeared. "What the fuck is the meaning of this?" he asked, thrusting his coveralls in her face. "Where's my clean pair, eh?"

He needed clean coveralls every day for his morning job at a Shell gas station. "Sorry, dear." Annie stammered. "I f-forgot —"

"Fucking airhead! You got my pants and shirt ready for Walmart?"

In the afternoons he restocked shelves. "Yes. Coffee, Ted?"

"Yeah," he said, throwing the coveralls at her feet. Soon, fucks and guitar chords were exploding from the bedroom.

The stained coveralls had to be laundered separately. Annie dashed out of the apartment and down to the basement, threw them into a machine and ran back to make coffee. Then she got on with supper, doubling the recipe for macaroni and cheese so that she wouldn't have to bake tomorrow.

At 7:30 p.m., dressed in jeans and a black shirt with leather fringes, Ted announced he was off and that he'd had it up to here with holding down three fucking jobs and no way would he eat fucking macaroni-cheese shit for the second day running. Annie listened with her head bent. After he'd slammed the apartment door, she called the children for supper.

When the dishes were washed she got out the ironing board and switched on the TV so the children could watch *Singin' in the Rain*. She watched with them, waiting for the scene she loved best: Gene Kelly, overflowing with love and hope and happiness as he splashed through rain puddles.

"Isn't that scene lovely, kids? So lovely!"

"Mom, are you crying?" Tara asked.

"Of course not. I've just got a bit of a cold."

When the children were in bed, she got out her mending. Every commercial TV channel pounded with murder and mayhem while the public television station was airing a special on how to invest your spare thousands. As the moderator droned about the importance of diversifying your portfolio, she reached for *The Vancouver Sun*, alternating between a torn hem and Letters to the Editor. One letter suggested that the Virgin Mary was merely the Christian substitute for the ancient Venus of Sacred Love, while Mary Magdalene was the substitute for the Venus of Profane Love, and that both these women were merely interchangeable representatives of a female archetype that had always been carried in the human unconscious. Now that Christianity was fading, the writer suggested, the dead Princess Diana was worshipped as the Virgin Mary while Madonna filled the role of Mary Magdalene.

She read the letter again. The writer was a Dr. E. Zaleski of West Vancouver.

West Vancouver, the richest municipality in Canada, was located on the north shore of Burrard Inlet, opposite her own area of the Downtown Eastside, Canada's most poverty-stricken community.

She found the telephone number and dialled.

"Hello?" said a woman's voice.

"Could I speak to Doctor Zaleski, please?"

"Doctor Enid Zaleski speaking."

For a second or two she was surprised into silence. She had expected a man, not a woman. "Did you have a letter published in *The Vancouver Sun* today?"

"Yes. Can I help you?"

"No, I just wanted to hear the voice of a total fucking stupido."

As she was replacing the telephone she heard a strange sound issuing from the earpiece but couldn't stop her hand's downward thrust. The telephone crashed into its cradle.

She waited for her usual high, but for the second time that day it didn't arrive. Drunken laughter erupted from the parking lot; the screech of traffic on East Hastings racked her nerves. She stood beside the kitchen window. Sunset was striking gold from the distant windows of West Vancouver, while her own area was suffused in a livid crimson that suggested the rickety boarding houses and stucco apartment blocks of the Downtown Eastside were going up in flames.

It was impossible to settle. Switching off the TV, she worked in silence, pushing a needle in and out of Brendan's torn jeans. The strange sound that had come out of the telephone began to torment her, and her stitching became erratic. She had used the phrase "total fucking stupido" on several occasions, and the recipient had always been satisfyingly upset.

A jab from the needle caused her to gasp in pain. Sucking at her thumb, she realised that she could no longer deny what she had heard pealing out of the telephone: laughter.

The laughter would not go away. It scraped along her nerves as she finished her mending. It followed her into the kitchen, harassing her while she made a cup of tea. It accompanied her into the bathroom and was still tormenting her when she tiptoed into the children's bedroom and checked their clenched little sleeping faces. As she loosened Brendan's grip on the blanky he wouldn't give up even though he was now eight years old, she knew that Enid Zaleski had been neither angered nor frightened by the anonymous call. Enid Zaleski had considered Annie's insult funny.

When she returned to the living room, she was trembling.

It was nearly 3:00 a.m. when Ted, his clothes stinking of cigarette smoke, staggered into the bedroom. After yanking open the window, he bellyflopped into bed and pitched into sleep as the roar of Hastings Street traffic ground around the bedroom walls. She knew better than to close the window again. After a gig, Ted said, he had to have his fresh air. Like a whale beached in its own foul shallows, he lay blowing beery smells from both ends.

When the alarm clock pointed to 3:25 and her nerves were in rags, she inched out of bed. Afraid to switch on a light, she used a flashlight to find Enid Zaleski's telephone number. She dialled.

"Hello?"

Taking a deep breath, Annie began breathing hoarsely into the mouthpiece.

The whistle blast that screamed down the line nearly took her eardrum out. She flung the telephone away, crying out against the pain and dropping to her knees, both hands flying to her mouth as she realised her cry might have woken Ted. Battling the urge to throw up, she replaced the telephone and crawled back to bed. Hours passed before she finally fell asleep.

Around noon, Ted dropped her off at Wilson's Tools. Leaning out of the Honda's side window he told her, "Be out here by five-past-five, stupido. I got fucking Benson's Foods at six."

"Y-y-yes, d-dear."

For once, he didn't take off immediately. Instead, his face crumpled and for an astonishing few seconds he seemed like a frightened little boy about to cry. Tears rushed into her eyes in response, but then he muttered, "Oh fuck!" and drew back. The Honda coughed down the road.

In the bare-looking main office (flowers and photos were discouraged) rows of women sat in front of computers. Annie's job involved processing the paperwork for the sales staff. Her ear was still painful, and soon, her right temple was throbbing a warning of an impending migraine. And whose fault was that? Enid Zaleski's.

By mid-afternoon, in spite of the dulling effects of Tylenol, she could no longer contain her rage. Betty, her supervisor, was leaving early and Annie asked if she could use the office telephone. That, she knew, was not available to the call-back service.

"Annie, you know Mr. Arnold says staff aren't allowed to make personal calls until after five."

"I can't do it at five. Ted won't be kept waiting."

Betty was a stocky, dark-haired woman with a no-nonsense manner. She said, "It won't kill him to wait two minutes."

"I can't tell him that. He's working three jobs."

"Christ, I hate it when women let their men walk all over them! You've had a college education, which is more than he's had. Why d'you let him treat you like a doormat?"

Annie's throat tightened. "Ted and I understand each other ..."

"Really? Is that why he calls you 'stupido.' Is that why you stammer when you talk to him?"

"You don't understand." Annie attempted to stop her voice from shaking. "We have a lot of expenses. And now we have to pay for dental checkups for the kids. I have to keep my budget in balance." No way would she mention that the free school breakfast program had been cut, and that sometimes her kids went to school with nothing in their stomachs.

"I'm sorry," Betty said, relenting. "All right, use the phone but make it short."

"You can't take on the whole world, Betty!"

"Right," Betty said. "So you start with one. You." The door closed behind her.

The telephone number was burned into Annie's memory. This time she did not place the receiver against her ear.

"Enid Zaleski speaking."

"You're a fucking asshole shithead stupido cunt!"

As she moved to replace the telephone, she heard Enid Zaleski say softly, "I'm truly sorry about your troubles."

Annie's hand halted in mid-air. She thrust her lips into the mouthpiece. "I don't have any troubles. You're the fucker with the troubles, fucking ignorant atheist stupido!"

"Are you a churchgoer?" Enid Zaleski asked mildly.

For a moment Annie was too startled to respond; then she shot back, "No, I'm not, but many good people are! Who the fucking hell are you to tell innocent people that Princess Diana was the Virgin Mary? A whore like her? Are you aware, you fucking bitch, that *The Vancouver Sun* is distributed throughout the whole of British Columbia? Have you even the faintest fucking idea (her voice filled with contempt) of the damage you've caused? And do you care? No, because that's what you do, isn't it? In love with your own fucking voices, that's the trouble with you motherfucking know-it-alls!"

"It's very sad that a mere opinion should upset you so much."

"You're the fucker who should be upset! That's the trouble, isn't it? You think the rest of us are all stupidos!"

"I don't think you're stupid, caller. As a matter of fact, I'd say you're an educated woman."

For the second time, Annie was too shocked to reply. She stammered, "F-f-fucking shit-faced liar!"

"But you do realize, don't you, that all I have to do is to press this little button, and I can discover your telephone number, who you are and where you live?"

"Don't give me that shit! This phone can't be traced by fucking star fucking sixty-nine!"

"You're out of date, caller. Haven't you heard of lasers?"

Fright silenced Annie immediately. Enid Zaleski lived in British Properties. People there could afford expensive gadgets.

The other woman's calm voice was saying, "You're obviously deeply troubled about something. I'm truly sorry about that."

Annie tried to say, "My fucking life is fine, thank you very much," but she only got as far as "My fucking life ..." and then her voice died.

"Are you married?"

"To a fine man!" Annie shouted, coming to life. "A hard worker!"

Enid Zaleski continued, "Then most likely you have children. Probably two, that's the average. I'm guessing you've got financial problems, especially with all the recent cuts to social programs. I'm guessing your man is the type who takes his worries out on his partner. I'm guessing you've had a decent education, but somehow you've lost any advantage that may have given you. Or maybe you got into this relationship when you were very young and now you're realizing that all you are is a household drudge and a man's punching bag ..."

Annie's scalp prickled. Goose bumps itched over her arms. "M-m-my husband has never hit me. N-Never." It was the truth. Ted had never struck her.

"When you look in the mirror, what do you see? A shabby woman? A despairing woman? Maybe the mirror shows nothing at all, only a blank where a woman should be. Or maybe it shows a woman who is enduring a living death ..."

Very carefully, Annie replaced the telephone.

Several times during the following three weeks she awoke to the sound of weeping. She would open her eyes to the stained wall where Ted had thrown a cup of coffee and think confusedly, Oh dear, there's a woman crying. Just as she was about to identify the voice, she would be wide awake and have to scramble to make breakfast.

She became absent-minded; Ted had to hold his left hand an inch from her nose and then punch the palm with his right fist — his signal that she was to watch her p's and q's. All the while, she waited fearfully for a call from Enid Zaleski, for surely the other woman would have used the laser to trace the telephone number.

After the fourth week when Enid Zaleski still hadn't called, Annie checked her housekeeping money, then bought a clay pot of African violets and placed it on her desk. The pink blossoms were like a family of bright little faces. Betty said nothing. Next day, another woman placed on her own desk a pot of trailing ivy whose silvery green leaves fell over the cold metal like a shower of little living stars. The following morning, another woman brought a big pot of tawny chrysanthemums and placed it on top of a filing cabinet so that the warm colours could be enjoyed by everyone. Slowly, a subtle perfume, reminiscent of fresh country meadows, quiet woods and restful gardens, drifted through the office. None of the executive staff said a word. Somewhere deep inside Annie, a fragile emotion stirred like a delicate plant reaching for the light.

Betty remarked, "Hey, Annie, you're looking better these days. You won the lottery?"

"As a matter of fact, I am feeling a bit better." Annie said, adding hesitantly, "Everybody's entitled to be treated decently, aren't they? Even stupid people are entitled to be treated decently."

"They are. But we know you're not stupid, don't we?" Betty said, staring hard at her. "A stupid person couldn't hold down your job."

"D'you really think so?"

"I know so."

Annie had not made one anonymous call since talking to Enid Zaleski. She now thought of the other woman as Enid. Obviously Enid was insightful and highly intelligent. She was also willing to admit she was wrong. Look how she'd listened, not interrupting, when she was told she was damaging people of faith. Clearly she had never thought of her letter's potential for harm, so it wasn't as if Annie had taken all and given nothing back. It had been an equal exchange.

Five weeks after the telephone call, Annie decided to contact Enid again. Maybe, for the first time since Ted had lost his full-time job at the shoe factory, she could have a female friend. Together, they could discuss the problems facing women with

young children. The first peal of the telephone, however, frightened her so badly that she hung up.

One week after that, she sat in Mr. Arnold's office waiting for
his instructions regarding the new sales compensation plan. She
had screwed up her courage and decided that tonight, while Ted
was out, she would telephone Enid. She would tell her that her
own name was Ann Gallagher, tell her that she was sorry about
her original phone call, tell her everything.

As the minutes ticked past, her bored gaze landed on a
National Post. The *Post* boasted that it was Canada's national
newspaper. Idly, she turned to the Letters page and saw a head-
line reading LETTER OF THE DAY. Beneath it was the caption,
VENUS, VIRGIN MARY, DIANA, MADONNA REPRESENT ANCIENT
FEMALE ARCHETYPES.

Enid Zaleski's letter had been printed in heavy black type
so that it stood out from the other letters. As if that weren't
enough, it was also enclosed within a heavy black rectangle,
signifying editorial approval, signifying that the editor was so
impressed with this particular letter that he wanted to make sure
no reader missed it. Enid Zaleski was the star of Letters to the
Editor, all across Canada, coast-to-coast.

Office workers cried out as a weeping Annie burst into the
main office, seized the pot of violets on her desk and hurled it
against a wall. Earth and broken clay exploded in all directions,
and a shard scraped the cheek of one of the women. Betty grabbed
Annie as she was reaching for something else to throw and
hustled her into a side office.

Her supervisor's mouth was opening and shutting as she spoke
into a telephone, but Annie couldn't hear because of her own

sobbing. Women in the main office were huddling together; frightened faces were watching through the connecting window. Then Betty was helping Annie into her jacket.

"The taxi will be here any minute," her white-faced supervisor told her. "It's not for me to say if you still have your job." Lifting a piece of paper, she scribbled on it and held it out. "Annie, for your sake, for your kids' sake, get some help! Here's the number of a good psychologist who does volunteer work at a transition house. Call her. Let me know how you're doing."

Enid Zaleski's name and phone number swam up through Annie's tears. As her supervisor watched in consternation, she tore the paper to shreds.

She was now lying on her bed in the empty apartment, staring with swollen eyes at the ceiling. Enid Zaleski was a fake, a forked-tongued trickster who had treated her with utter contempt. What did you do with these arrogant people who treated you as if you were a total stupido?

After a while she reached for the telephone directory. Not for the number. For the address.

Right in the middle of supper, she thought about fingerprints. Brendan, who was starting to look like his father, was whining about having macaroni and cheese again. Ted had already had his say and was bitterly shovelling macaroni into his mouth. Fingerprints, she thought. Enid Zaleski was cunning. She would certainly have any missile checked for fingerprints.

"More macaroni," Ted ordered.

Today the manager at the gas station where he worked part-time had bawled him out in front of a customer, and Ted had had what he called "a few beers." As his bloodshot glare found her face, he began slamming his right fist into his left palm. The casserole was two inches from his plate. "C-c-certainly, dear," she said, scrambling up.

Later, he sprawled in front of the television set, sucking on one bottle of beer after another. Afterwards, she helped him into bed, where he passed out. When his snoring became regular, she hid warm clothes and a pair of cotton gloves in the bathroom closet, together with a sketch of the route to Number Ten Heather Gardens and a box of Tylenol she'd purchased earlier. Then she slid into bed, listening to Ted's snores and waiting for the clock dial to register 3:00 a.m. At 3:05 she inched out of bed, eased the car keys off the dresser, changed in the bathroom and slipped out of the apartment.

A tainted wind lifted her hair as she tiptoed into the moonlit parking lot. Their apartment was on the ground floor and their own parking spot was directly in front of their bedroom window. She unlocked the Honda and placed the Tylenol — her alibi in case Ted woke up and found she'd left the apartment — on the passenger seat. Pulling on her gloves, she tiptoed to the broken curb, selected a big lump of concrete and placed it beside the Tylenol. Slowly, carefully, she released the brake and guided the car backwards, struggling with the wheel until at last she had manoeuvred the Honda a good distance from the apartment. Then she climbed inside and started the car.

At this hour there was less traffic on East Hastings, but a few girls, paired for safety, their baby faces garish with makeup, were huddling in the doorways of the shabby stores. She drove carefully, for she was out of practice. Fifteen minutes later she had crossed the Lions Gate Bridge, driven through the Park Royal shopping area and begun negotiating a tree-lined road hair-pinning up between landscaped gardens and beautiful homes.

Heather Gardens was a cul-de-sac near the top of British Properties, the most exclusive part of West Vancouver. She drove past the No Exit sign, pulling into the curb when she saw an ornate brass Ten gleaming from a carved signboard. Switching off the engine, she rolled down her window.

The profound silence that only money can buy hallowed the richly perfumed air. Enid Zaleski's house, pearled by moonlight, stood at the end of a long driveway edged by gardenia bushes starred with white blossoms. Four tall windows on the upper floor were beautified by shutters and flower-filled window boxes; on the ground floor, an imposing entrance door was flanked by two windows on the left, while to the right an enormous picture window glittered an imperial black. It offered what looked like several thousand dollars worth of plate glass.

She drove to the end of the cul-de-sac and parked. For awhile she crouched in her seat, tense in case a light came on in a window, drawing in deep breaths and exhaling slowly in an attempt to steady the banging of her heart. Far below, on the southern shore of Burrard Inlet, the Downtown Eastside glittered within its neons. The lump of concrete was a misshapen shadow beside her.

The Honda exploded into life. Flooring the accelerator, she stormed towards Number Ten and careened up the driveway. She stopped the car, grabbed the lump of concrete and leaped out. Racing towards the picture window and bringing back her arm, she flung the concrete with all her strength. The window shattered. She hurled herself back into the Honda and reversed.

The Honda crashed into the bushes and she put it into forward and screeched down Heather Gardens through the stop sign.

She couldn't catch her breath; she was icy cold in spite of the warm night. Pulling into the curb, she opened her door and threw up on the road. She was trembling from head to foot. But Enid Zaleski would also be trembling this very minute, standing in her living room and staring at the ruined window, knowing very well who had inflicted the damage but not knowing how to prove it, for the gloves would have acted as a barrier to finger-prints. Annie Gallagher was no stupido!

The Lions Gate Bridge arched before her, Burrard Inlet glis-tening its oily black satins far below. Soon, she was back in the Downtown Eastside. As the small shops slid past, she relived again and again the destruction of the window, a destruction that proved she was not a helpless victim but an autonomous being who could and would defend herself against those who treated her as if she was a nothing.

She drew up some distance from their parking spot, then switched off and leaned to retrieve the Tylenol. For a frightening few seconds she couldn't find it, but then her fingers closed around the box and she thrust it into a pocket before pushing the Honda back into place. It was difficult to lock the car door without slamming it, but somehow she managed. When she turned away, however, something slapped against her legs, releasing an exquisite perfume. Trapped in the rear fender was a branch of gardenia, extravagant with blossom. She threw it away before slipping into the apartment and undressing in the bathroom.

In spite of the open window, the bedroom stank of beer and cigarettes. Ted was snoring on his belly, arms and legs occupying all four corners of the bed. Leaving the door ajar, she inched into the remaining space.

Presently, she became aware of an exquisite perfume from outside. She didn't dare close the window. Clamping a hand over her mouth, she fought the sob trying to force its way up her throat.

She was giving the children their breakfast when the telephone pealed. She picked it up.

"Ann Gallagher," said Enid Zaleski, "your licence plate was in my driveway. I traced you via the Internet. How about coming to my house and talking?"

Annie's breath left her. Seconds ticked past. Ted shouted from the bathroom, "That for me?"

"Could you be here by ten o'clock? The local blue bus passes Heather Gardens once an hour. You could catch the nine-forty from Park Royal."

"I'm talking to you, stupido!" shouted Ted.

"Tell your husband you've got an appointment with Doctor Zaleski. It won't be a lie." Enid Zaleski said.

"You fucking deaf?" Ted bellowed. The children cowered as he strode out of the bedroom. "Gimmee that fucking phone!"

"I'll c-catch the n-nine-f-forty," Annie gasped into the mouthpiece. Replacing the telephone on the stand she told Ted, "D-d-doctor's appointment. Women's troubles. I'll take the bus."

"Fucking right you will! Fucking right!"

"Yes," she said, and reached blindly for a chair because the decision had taken so much out of her that she had to sit down.

ACKNOWLEDGEMENTS

MY VERY GRATEFUL THANKS go to writers Betty Keller, Deanna Lueder and Heather Waddell for their unstinting help and encouragement. Grateful thanks are also due to Ian Zweig for designing my website.

"Country of Evil" first appeared in *Event Magazine* in 2003; in a slightly different version, it won that magazine's creative non-fiction prize and was subsequently a finalist in the Western Canadian Magazine Awards in 2004.